'Do y̶o̶u̶ ̶t̶h̶i̶n̶k̶ ̶I̶'̶m̶ in some damned gigolo?'

'I don't know the first thing about you,' Molly answered.

'No one said you had to pay my way.' Tell's voice was hard.

'Oh, I suppose cowboys have lots and lots of money and camp out when they come to Acapulco just for the fun of it!'

'What do you do, ask to see a man's bank balance before going out with him? You're no better than a trashy gold-digger!'

Dear Reader

Whatever the weather this summer, come with us to four places in the sun. In this collection, we offer you the romance you love – with a dash of the exotic. . .the hazy heat and shimmering sands of Tunisia. . .the colourful glamour of Acapulco Beach. . .the tropical beauty of Indonesia. . .the timeless mystique of Egypt. A magical tour of sensual delight, with four happy endings along the way! Something sultry from Mills & Boon. . .

The Editor

Barbara McMahon, her husband and teenage daughter share their home with one dog and four cats in the San Francisco Bay area. She works for a computer software company, writing on weekends and evenings. A love for romances and happy endings led to a strong desire to create stories she'd like to read herself. In earlier days she visited exotic locales when she flew for an international airline, and now uses some of these places in her books. Her hobbies are reading, skiing, and writing.

Recent titles by the same author:

ONE LOVE FOREVER
LOVE'S UNEXPECTED TURN

MISS PRIM AND PROPER

BY

BARBARA McMAHON

MILLS & BOON LIMITED
ETON HOUSE   18-24 PARADISE ROAD
RICHMOND   SURREY   TW9 1SR

*First published in Great Britain 1993
by Mills & Boon Limited*

© Barbara McMahon 1993

*Australian copyright 1993
Philippine copyright 1993
This edition 1993*

ISBN 0 263 77984 X

*Set in Times Roman 10½ on 12 pt.
93-9307-51086 C*

Made and printed in Great Britain

CHAPTER ONE

MOLLY almost hugged herself with glee, giddy with delight. Here she was, Molly Spencer, who a month ago had faced unemployment, dwindling savings and bleak prospects, now standing on a terrace overlooking beautiful Acapulco Bay. The soft corals and pink that painted the evening sky reflected on the calm, shimmering sea. Evening breezes were cool after the sultry heat of the day, blowing in gently from the west. The scent of the sea washed across her skin in a tangible caress. Across the bay lights were blinking on in the high-rise glass and steel hotels that encircled the shore.

Her eyes delighted in the sights before her, as she stood at the edge of the terrace, leaning lightly against the railing that held her from the edge. It was wonderful, heady. In her wildest imaginings she'd never pictured herself in Acapulco.

Behind her she could hear the soft murmur of her new boss, talking on the phone to someone in Los Angeles. No other sounds marred the peaceful and serene setting. Molly's eyes again skimmed the horizon, the bay, the city in the distance. It was all so magical—would she ever get tired of looking at the view? Maybe by the end of their stay, but she secretly doubted it.

She turned slowly to survey her own particular bit of Acapulco. Las Casitas D'Oro Hotel was enchanting. Built on the steep side of a hill, each room or suite opened to a private terrace, with its own private swimming-pool.

She was in a two-room suite, hers to the left, her employer's to the right. The large flagstone terrace united the two rooms. A tall cinder-block wall, painted blue and white, divided their terrace from the room to their left. A half-wall to the right separated them from the open hillside. The large, kidney-shaped pool invited her to swim. The pool was to be shared with Beverley, no one else.

Molly's grin threatened to split her face. This was the most wonderful setting she'd ever seen! And pure luck was the sole reason she was here.

He was in the shadows and she didn't see him until he moved. He slipped easily around the wall beside Beverley's room, pausing at the gate that separated their terrace from the wild, untamed land of the hillside. Thrusting open the wooden gate, he walked boldly on to the patio as if he owned the place, a stack of fluffy blue and white towels in his arms.

Startled, Molly straightened up, looking at the man, glancing into the room where Beverley talked on the phone; her back was to the window, and she was clearly engrossed in her conversation. No help there. Molly looked again at the intruder. Did she need help?

He stood just inside the colourful blue gate, blending in with the shadows of the early evening. The light from the rooms spilled across part of the patio, making the spot where he stood, just outside, seem darker, mysterious.

Though probably not much over six feet tall, from Molly's diminutive five feet two he seemed to tower over her. Tall and well-built, without any fat. She could attest to that since, except for tight cut-off jeans riding low on his narrow hips, he had nothing else on.

She blinked, a curious fluttering sensation in the pit of her stomach.

'Who are you?' Molly asked, stepping away from the railing.

His hair was long, shaggy, dark in the fading light, and he hadn't shaved for a couple of days, yet it only enhanced his rugged masculinity. He was barefoot. His shoulders were broad and muscular, his chest developed, tapering to a strong, flat stomach. Muscular legs, spread apart, firmly anchored him to the patio.

Molly took a breath, her eyes involuntarily drawn to his chest, trailing down to his tight cut-offs. Raw sex in tight jeans, she thought involuntarily and her senses tingled as awareness of his animal magnetism threatened to engulf her.

She was suddenly hot, and it wasn't only because of the instant flush when she realised where her thoughts were heading. Compared to the man before her, she was terribly overdressed. The hot, sultry climate required fewer articles of clothing and she still wore the suit she'd travelled in, which had been so appropriate in Los Angeles.

She took a step closer and peered up, trying to see his face in the dim light, trying to ignore the strong desire to feast her eyes on his body, schooling her features to reveal none of her thoughts, trying to ignore the sudden longing to touch him that quivered in her fingertips.

At the sound of her voice, he looked up, looked up and stared at her as she stood silhouetted by the setting rays of the sun. The fading light threw shadows across the planes of his face, his eyes were fathomless and mysterious. His lips twitched as he scanned her and he strolled over past one of the chairs, carelessly dropping the towels as he passed, staring down at her.

'You just arrive?' He looked slowly down her body again, as if amazed at the superfluous garments worn in such a hot climate. Molly's nerves tingled as his gaze touched her breasts, moved to her hips and passed, continued down.

'Yes, I just arrived. Do you work here?'

He shook his head slowly, his eyes roaming freely over her trim figure.

'If you don't work here, what are you doing?' She had to take charge of the exchange; she was too distracted by the odd feeling in her breast at his lingering glance. He was trespassing on her patio and she wanted him to leave.

'I'm looking at you, right now, darlin',' he said, grinning, his eyes clashing with hers. She could see the gleam of his white teeth. He shifted a little and took a step closer.

Molly frowned at his teasing tone and when he moved she could see him better, but wasn't reassured. His eyes were still in shadow, hooded by dark brows, a two-day growth of beard covered his lean cheeks. Yet her interest soared. Who was he and why was he here? He looked tired, scruffy, dishevelled; but not like a vagrant, more like a man on his own, removed from daily routines, doing just as he damned well pleased.

'You're staying in these rooms? I brought you some towels.'

Molly had a moment of doubt. The towels looked right. The entire hotel was done in blue and white, its trademark. But the man didn't look right. None of the hotel staff she'd seen thus far had been out of uniform. The bright blue uniform of Las Casitas D'Oro.

This man looked more like Pancho Villa, wild lawless, free. Definitely not a hotel employee, out to please the guests. He looked as if he only pleased himself.

He took a step closer and Molly could see him in the light from the room. She met his eyes with a shock. They were a light silvery grey. Surprising in one so dark. His skin was tanned a dusky bronze, his hair inky in the darkening sky.

'Thank you. Goodnight.'

He smiled again. 'Want me to go, do you?' His eyes danced down at her as he stepped closer, placing his hands on his hips. He looked immovable.

Feeling flustered and rude, Molly none the less stood her ground. 'I won't keep you from...' From what? He'd said he didn't work for the hotel—what was he doing here?

Her eyes flickered to the short wall to her right. Beyond it was the open hillside. Wild, uncultivated land, restricted to no one. A thief could easily stalk these rooms. In and out fast. Was he here to see who had just checked in?

'I think you'd better leave.' She tried to make her voice as forceful and confident as she could.

'Your first trip to Acapulco?' he asked, ignoring her command.

'Yes, it is, and this is a private patio.' If he refused to leave, what would she do? She hated to cause a scene.

He smiled at that, his fists resting solidly on his hips. He looked her over indolently, from head to feet, his light eyes dancing in his face as he met her gaze again.

Molly flushed, her skin instantly warm. Suddenly convinced he saw through the trim blue skirt and silky white blouse that hugged her figure, she was startled at the awareness of her own sexuality that he raised. She tilted her head up to meet his gaze, standing her ground. He was the trespasser, not she. He was the one who should be embarrassed at being asked to go.

'Are you leaving?' She blinked through her glasses, wishing illogically that she had worn something soft and feminine. Wishing she had combed through her hair. Wishing he'd look at her with longing, rather than amusement.

How stupid—she was here to work, not flirt with the first man that happened by.

'*Señorita*, here I come to welcome you to this beautiful city and all you want to do is have me leave. I can show you the attractions of Acapulco, guide you to all the places tourists want to see, fill your days with wonderful sights to see, and fill your nights with warm, loving memories to dream about for years to come.'

His voice was like a dark melody, piercing through to her heart. If she closed her eyes, she felt she could listen to him forever. The tone was low, smooth, sexy, the words seductive. She shook her head. What was she thinking of?

'I'm sorry, I have already planned my trip. Thank you for the towels. Do you want a tip?' She wanted him to go, yet he wouldn't budge.

'Are you sure you don't need a guide? How about to the beaches? I'm sure you'd look great in a

swimsuit, and I know where the best beaches are.'
Amusement was evident in his tone.

This was getting out of hand. Molly stepped closer,
a look of pure determination on her face.

'Look, *señor*, this is a private terrace and if you
don't leave, I'll . . . I'll call the hotel security force and
have you removed.' She stalked over to him, in-
tending to pass him and head for her room. If he
wouldn't leave, she would. But he casually stepped
between her and the door.

The terrace narrowed where he stood, the half-wall
on one side, the pool on the other. She stopped abruptly, touched by a flash of fear. She didn't know
who this man was, but he was between her and safety.
He was tall, strongly built, the muscles of his shoulders
and arms developed from hard work. His skin was
dark, smooth and supple, except for the black hair
that covered his chest, moving down to dive beneath
the waistband of his cut-off jeans.

Molly jerked her head up when she realised where
her eyes were heading, confused when she again met
his eyes. He was laughing at her!

'What is it you want?' Her voice quavered slightly.

'Only to be of service to the lovely *señorita*.' His
voice mocked, his eyes never left hers.

She was annoyed, and just a little hurt. She was
not lovely, but plain. Her glasses enabled her to see,
but they were not fashionable. She bought them for
economy, not looks. Her dark, wavy hair was scraped
back from her face in a serviceable but unremarkable
french braid. She looked just as she was, a girl with
no money, who had to work for a living and had no
time for frivolity or frivolous things.

She didn't need some stranger mocking her on her looks. She didn't need him here at all. Why wouldn't he leave?

'Do you want money?'

'I'm insulted. Here I offer to show you the sights and you want to pay me.' He stood straight, arms falling to his side. It did not make him any less formidable. 'If I wanted payment, it wouldn't be in money.'

Her imagination let her know what he would want payment in. Her heart began pounding and she turned and walked around the pool. She would go into her room and shut the door. Maybe she'd even call for the hotel security. She was halfway around when she realised he was pacing her, on the room side of the pool, slowly, steadily, matching step for step. When she reached the other end, he would be there, cutting off her escape to her room.

She paused, feeling foolish. Were they to dance around the pool all night? A touch of anger coursed through her. He was playing games while she was only trying to do her job.

One of the reasons Beverley Sampson had hired her was to keep her life free from interruptions while she worked on another of her biographies. Molly took her work very seriously. She would not be bested by this stranger. Failure to remove this man would not augur well for her ability to handle the position. And she desperately wanted to keep the position.

When Molly stopped, the stranger did not. He continued around the pool, his eyes never leaving her. She wished for a moment he'd trip and fall into the water, but he stayed clear of the edge. His eyes remained fixed on her.

Coming up to her, he took her arm gently in one hand and slowly moved her to the railing. For a moment she thought he meant to toss her over, but he simply turned her around and motioned to the far end of the bay.

Leaning over, he put his head close to hers, pointing across the bay.

'That's where the cruise ships dock. There's none in port tonight, but there'll be some soon. They're very pretty, all in white, with flags flying and bright lights at night. Sometimes you can almost hear the music from the ships, if the wind is right.'

He was so close to her that she could feel the heat from his body. The breeze cooled her skin through her silk shirt, but the warmth from his skin permeated. She concentrated on the sights he was pointing out to her, conscious of his hand still on her arm, of the tingling sensation moving through her body as his touch energised. Conscious of his face, only inches from hers, she could see him clearly from the corner of her eye. His voice was soft, melodious, velvety in the growing darkness.

He pointed out each hotel on La Contessa Beach by name, first the soaring Continental, then the elegant Plaza International, and the old El Presidente. She licked her lips and tried to differentiate the various buildings, following his hand as he showed her. Her breathing grew difficult. Slowly, unobtrusively, she parted her lips to breathe better. Her heart was tripping double time in her breast and the warmth she experienced earlier was growing uncomfortable.

'It's too dark now to see,' he said sadly. 'I'll have to come again and point them out to you in the daytime.'

'N-no.' Was that her voice, so breathless? She cleared her throat and stepped back. Could she make it to her room now?

'No, I don't think that's a good idea.'

'Ah, but I do. I think we should get to know each other. I can still show you the sights.'

'Look, *señor*, I'm here to work. Not to go sight-seeing, not to mingle with the na——' She stopped, appalled at her rudeness.

He laughed softly, mockingly in the dark. She could see the faint light spilling from the room gleam on his white teeth. His dark colouring was almost sinister in the night-time.

'Not mingle with the natives, eh? Well, it's early days yet, and who knows what you'll see and do here in Mexico? But I'm not Mexican.'

'You're not?' She was embarrassed.

'No, darlin', I'm from Texas. But I've been to Acapulco before and can show you around.'

She blinked, staring at him. She should have known. Mexico was a foreign country, and his English was the same as hers, except for a slight accent. If she'd not been so worried about his being here, if she'd not been so conscious of his body and her reaction to it, she would have caught that.

And it was evident he was brash enough to be a Texan. Was he a cowboy?

'Wherever you're from, I don't have time to see things—I'm here to work!' Molly was very certain. She stepped casually back another foot. If she could keep him talking, she could move closer to her room and make a dash for it.

'One can work too hard.'

She stared up at him, her heart suffocating in its pounding. Slowly he leaned over and gently brushed her lips with his fingertips.

'Go to your room now, little one, and lock your door at night. Who knows if the wolves will come over the hill.'

'Wolves?'

He shrugged, and moved past her, heading for the wooden gate in the half-wall that separated the terrace from the open hillside. 'Who knows? There are wolves around everywhere.'

'You should know that,' she muttered.

His smile at her as he went through the gate made her wonder if he heard her.

She watched him but in only seconds he was lost to the darkness. She didn't hear him move across the ground, but she knew he was gone. She felt curiously bereft.

Turning for one last look at the enchanting setting of Acapulco Bay, she slowly moved to her room.

Beverley was still on the phone, so Molly switched on her lights and began unpacking the few clothes she'd brought with her. Speculating on who her visitor might have been, she put away the dresses and cotton trousers. Was he a man holidaying at the hotel? He didn't look the type. Most of the people she'd seen as they drove into this exclusive resort were well dressed, properly turned out. Her stranger on the patio didn't strike her as proper at all. He looked as if he scoffed at conventions, ignored rules he didn't make. But was he a guest? He'd never said.

She wondered if she'd see him again. Probably not. And if he saw her in the daylight, would he be sorry? He'd been flattering, but the light was dim and kind.

Molly had no illusions. She was nice-looking, but not pretty. Kept herself well, but with inexpensive clothes. Life had not been easy for her and she was very careful with her money. She would not be caught with nothing the way her mother had been.

This job with Beverley Sampson had been a gift from heaven. Molly smiled at her good fortune as she hung up the last of her cotton dresses, put the suitcase in the bottom of the spacious cupboard. Her old company had merged with another and Molly's job had been eliminated. She'd only had two more weeks of work when she applied for secretary to Beverley Sampson.

Beverley had written over a dozen biographies of famous people. She was well known in literary circles and had been unexpectedly left without a secretary when hers had eloped. Molly had fitted the bill perfectly.

And now they were in Acapulco for at least a month, to finish the draft of her latest work so that Beverley could send it to her publishers.

When Beverley had told Molly they would be a month in Mexico, Molly had expected a small house or apartment on a back-street, something inexpensive. Instead, they had two rooms at one of Mexico's most expensive resorts. She'd never dreamed of such a place and delighted in each new discovery.

But when Molly went to bed that night it was not the excitement of her new job or the luxuries of Las Casitas D'Oro that claimed her attention, but the image of dancing grey eyes, broad shoulders and shaggy black hair. She smiled wistfully, wishing she might see him once again, wondering who he was.

CHAPTER TWO

MOLLY awoke early the next morning, anticipation and happiness welling up. She was in Mexico! Starting a new job in a wonderful location. Anxious to greet the day, she hurried through dressing, donning white cotton trousers and a bright yellow top. Brushing her hair back, she quickly clasped it into a serviceable french braid. It was hot and heavy in the warm morning, but kept most of her hair off her neck.

Sliding open her door, she stepped out on to the patio. Involuntarily her eyes were drawn to the gate where her mysterious visitor from last night had disappeared. Illogically, she was disappointed he was not there, though there was no reason to expect him.

Glancing at the beauty of the bay, she walked casually over to the half-wall, sweeping her gaze across the open hillside. She saw only wild bushes, rocks and an occasional burst of yellow or red wildflowers. There was no path, no indication that anyone had walked across the ground last night.

Where had he come from, and where had he gone? The questions teased her mind as she forced herself away, across to the wrought-iron railing that gave way to the view she had so loved last night. The sky was clear and blue; the sun's rays sparkled on the glittering high-rises lining the distant beach, danced on the deep blue water.

Molly remembered the mysterious stranger's touch as she gazed over sights he'd pointed out last night.

17

She could almost feel his fingers on her arm, the warmth of his breath near her face, the sensuous touch of his fingers on her lips. It was almost as if he were there.

She turned slightly, expectantly, disappointed to find she was still alone.

Glancing over her shoulder, she saw the door to Beverley's room was still closed. Beside the pool, a large tray with covered baskets and a coffee carafe rested on one of the small tables. Molly investigated.

Rolls, croissants and pastries nestled in the baskets, still warm in their cosy. The coffee was fragrant and hot. She poured a large cup and took a croissant. Wandering back to the railing, she munched as she gazed over the view, her mind drifting, her eyes enjoying the beauty of the scene.

The sliding door drew her attention and Molly turned to greet her employer. Beverley Sampson emerged from her room the way a bird might emerge from a nest, looking around her, her eyes dark, and darting hither and yon.

'Good morning, Molly, how did you sleep? I always sleep poorly the first night in a new place. Though I wouldn't call this a new place—I've stayed here many times before. But I guess it takes some adjustment to get used to a different bed from the one you are used to. Did you sleep well? How do you like the view? No matter what room I get here the view is always the same and I know I can count on it.'

Beverley smiled vaguely at Molly, obviously expecting no answer, as she hurried over to the rolls and coffee. She was tiny, barely five feet tall, but bubbly and lively. Molly thought she had to be in her fifties, but her hair was light and touched up and Molly wasn't sure.

She'd been a shock to Molly, who had been expecting a writer to be quiet and thoughtful. Beverley was just the opposite, lively, talkative, given to blurting things out without thought, and without fear of consequences. Molly had never been around anyone quite like her, and found it disconcerting at times. She hoped in time she'd get used to her new boss.

This morning, however, she merely smiled and went to sit in the chair near the table.

'I slept fine, thank you. The croissants are delicious.' She offered the basket to Beverley, settling back to enjoy breakfast on the sunny patio.

'Mmm, I always like breakfast here. No matter what time you get up, it's waiting. I often wonder if they put it out the night before, but then how could the rolls stay so warm? Don't you love the coffee? It seems richer than what we have in the States, don't you think? I love it, especially with milk.'

Beverley took a roll and turned to look at the view, a pleased expression on her face. Molly watched her uncertainly, not sure of what her next duties would be. Beverley had been somewhat vague when explaining her duties to her.

'I want someone to type for me, put up with my thinking out loud. Do some research for facts, dates, and so on. Help with the locals. So often they want more time than I want to give. Do you speak Spanish? No, well, never mind. I speak it quite well; I grew up on the border and knew as much Spanish as English when I started school. Any questions?'

Molly smiled, remembering her interview. Beverley had done most of the talking, Molly not able to get a word in. But Beverley had been satisfied and hired her.

'I want to go into Acapulco for a few things this morning,' Beverley said, looking at her secretary. 'Want to go? You can browse around, shop a little. Might not get out for a few days once we get started on the book. Did you bring cooler clothes?' She looked at Molly's trousers. 'It gets very hot here and humid. I don't like the air-conditioner running all the time. You should get some things that will be cooler. I always wear shorts and light tops when working.'

Molly nodded. Knowing she'd be able to pick up a few things for less money in Mexico than in Los Angeles, she had purposely not bought anything suitable for such a hot climate. She had some money saved that she would use. But she wouldn't use it all. It always paid to have some in reserve. One never knew what the future would bring and Molly wanted to be prepared no matter what.

Beverley rented one of the colourful blue and white jeeps from the hotel. She insisted on driving, but told Molly she could use it whenever she wanted in the future.

The ride down the hillside from the hotel was hair-raising from Molly's point of view. The jeep had no door, and she cinched her seatbelt tight. Beverley drove with wild abandon, handling the car like a racing driver, screeching around corners, flooring the accelerator on the straight ways and acting as though she were on a thrill ride at an amusement park.

Molly hung on to the frame, the asphalt whizzing by at an alarming rate as Beverley chatted non-stop. She pointed out the various sights along the drive to Molly, indicating where they would turn off to use the beach club belonging to the hotel, indicating where friends of hers lived, and where Molly should drive one day to see the other side of the hill, the rural setting of the natives to Acapulco.

Slowing decorously once in the city limits, Beverley found a car park and stopped abruptly.

'Exciting place, Acapulco. I love it. I come here as much as I can. Writing can be done anywhere, so why not a place I love? I have some errands and know you'd like to look around. We'll meet for lunch at one. Right here, don't be late. I don't like people to be late.'

With a friendly, bird-like smile, Beverley jumped down from the jeep and scurried down the main street.

Molly watched with startled eyes as her employer disappeared from view. She was on her own. She looked around the busy street, the crowds spilling into the stores and shops. Feeling somewhat guilty that she wasn't working, she slowly climbed down from the jeep and picked her way through the gravel to the pavement.

Looking both ways, she saw the main thoroughfare was lined with shops of all sizes displaying their colourful wares in large windows and on racks lining the pavement. Everything was available. She began walking, watching the people, window-shopping, absorbing the sights and sounds so foreign to her. Colourful ponchos, decorated sombreros and wooden figurines were set up to lure the tourist. The friendly shopkeepers greeted everyone and urged them to try their shop.

Most of the people she passed were scantily dressed, bathing suits being the attire of choice. Short shorts, skimpy tops, and bare feet were everywhere. Molly began to feel positively overdressed in her white cotton trousers and lemon-yellow top.

Spanish was loud and rampant around her as exuberant Mexicans greeted each other in passing and stopped to talk. She also caught snatches of German, French and another language she couldn't guess. Once or twice she heard English.

'Obviously come shopping so you can fit in with the rest of us.' A warm, familiar voice sounded over her left ear.

Molly spun around, and there he was, her mysterious stranger from last night. Only inches away. He had shaved, she noticed immediately, and his skin was smooth now. She gazed at it, wondering what it would feel like if he kissed her...

Shocked at her thoughts, she darted a glance up at him. His eyes laughed down at her, and she looked away quickly, flustered. He hadn't read her mind, had he? She was afraid to look at him again.

Taking her arm, he turned her back in the direction she'd been going and fell into step beside her. She felt his warm, hard fingers through the thin cotton of her blouse, firm against her arm, causing the most peculiar constriction to her breathing. She looked straight ahead, but saw nothing, only a swirl of colour. What was the matter with her?

She chanced a glance at her companion, noting his broad shoulders, bronzed in the morning sun. His navy blue shorts were tight and fitted him like a second skin. No cut-offs today. His legs were long and muscular beneath the edge of the material, bronzed like the rest of him. Was he that colour all over?

Again she felt the heat spread through her. She'd better watch where her thoughts were leading. Was this what Mexico did to people, let them forget all their inhibitions? She never had thoughts like these about the men at her former office. She peeked up at his face and found his eyes dancing down at hers.

'I like looking at you, too,' he said audaciously.

She stopped and faced him, jerking her arm from his hand. 'I never said that!' she protested strongly, guilty because she did like looking at him. But he didn't need to know that.

He smiled. 'You can't keep your eyes off me.'

'Only because I can't believe you'd be downtown dressed like that.'

He wore no top and her eyes were drawn again and again to the muscles of his shoulders and chest. When he moved, they moved, fascinating her. His hair was shaggy, almost to his broad shoulders, yet on him it looked good. In fact, everything about him looked good. He was tall and well-built and Molly found him disturbingly sexy.

'Look around you—everyone dresses like this here. Thought that's why you were here—to get some clothes to fit in. You're still overdressed.'

He looked at her shirt, long cotton trousers, his gaze doing strange things to Molly's equilibrium. She remembered his comment from last night, and the feeling he'd given her. Her pulse fluttered. She was already warm, growing hotter and sticky in the humid air.

That was her problem. The weather was hot and humid. It had nothing to do with the man standing before her.

She turned away and looked at the others on the street with real attention. He was right; she did look overdressed by comparison. Mostly she saw skin, em-

barrassing amounts of skin. The revealing bikinis
worn by the tourists were mere scraps of colour, barely
within decency. The men on the pavements were in
shorts or swimming-trunks. Here and there a bright
shirt covered sun-reddened skin, but, for the most
part, the tourists were scantily clothed.

The natives of Acapulco, however, were more
properly dressed, the men in cotton trousers and white
shirts, the women in bright skirts and loose-fitting
peasant blouses.

In comparison to the other tourists, at least, her
unknown acquaintance was more closely in tune than
she.

She glanced back, surprised to find his eyes firmly
on her. With all the lovely women flaunting their
tanned bodies, it was a wonder he could spare a second
glance in her direction.

She pushed her glasses firmly in place and tilted her
head a little. Just what did he want? 'I was going to
look for some shorts,' she admitted reluctantly.

'And a swimsuit?' he asked, his eyes flicking down
her body, back to her eyes. 'You should get your hair
cut—it's too hot here for long hair.'

'I'm here to work, not play. I can put it up if it gets
too hot.'

'Suit yourself. Come on.' He steered her into one
of the open-fronted shops. Racks of colourful clothes
ranged deep into the interior. The pinks and blues were
vibrant, the yellows deep and bright. Green, purple,
rose, the colours swirled into a kaleidoscope of hues.

Molly looked eagerly at the displays. She could get
a few things, and maybe a swimsuit. She had only
brought an old black one-piece which she hadn't worn
much; she didn't usually have much time for going to

a beach. But here, even if she only had a few minutes each day, she could use the pool.

A saleswoman approached Molly, a polite smile on her face. When she saw the man beside her, her smile broadened, and the woman picked up her pace. Her eyes never left the face of Molly's companion.

Molly glanced at him again. He was something to draw the eye. She scanned the store quickly, noticing several women watching him as they pretended to examine clothes. A small feeling of awareness grew within her. He was more man than she knew how to handle. No wonder all the women were watching him. He was the type that dreams were made of.

Dreams for others, not for her. She knew her limitations and her future. She would not tie herself down with some Adonis with no money, no future, as her mother had. She knew the heartache and despair such actions could cause. Molly would be very cautious before letting herself be drawn to a man, no matter how good-looking.

'*Buenos días, señorita*, may I help you?'

'I'd like to look around first,' Molly said, gesturing at the colourful racks.

'Of course. In the back there are stalls.' She nodded to Molly, her eyes on the tall bronzed man, her smile seductive and welcoming.

Molly felt a prick of jealousy. Surprised at herself, she frowned and moved away, going slowly through the shop, examining the shorts, skirts, and festive sundresses. She loved the bright colours, and the casual, flowing loose lines. Her budget was limited, but she should be able to find something to suit her.

'Try this.'

A pretty hot-pink swimsuit was dangled before her. 'The colour will look good on you.'

'There's not enough to it—how would you know?' she protested. The suit was a two-piece, and looked small enough for a child.

'Do you see any others that are more to your liking?' His eyes always laughed at her.

Molly was flustered. In truth, all the suits were skimpy. 'Maybe another store.' She hesitated.

Without a word, he took her arm and propelled her to the back, gently shoving her into one of the stalls.

'I never knew a woman yet who didn't at least like to try things on.' He dropped the suit in her hands and yanked the cloth curtain closed.

Molly frowned. She normally didn't do anything like this. Who was he?

Suddenly feeling reckless and daring, she stepped out of her clothes and pulled on the suit. 'I can't wear this!' she said as she saw herself in the mirror.

The curtain slid open and he met her eyes in the mirror, then dropped to study her reflection. The bright pink of the suit deepened the pink in her cheeks, making the pale skin of her body seem whiter. The bikini-top plunged low, the swell of her breasts rounded above the fabric. The pants were low-cut, scarcely giving her decency. Her stomach was flat, her hips flared and her legs tapered beneath the satiny material.

Smouldering grey eyes clashed with hers in the mirror, as he drew a finger across the top of the bikini pants. Molly's stomach contracted sharply and her breath caught in her throat.

'You need a tan, darlin'. The suit is perfect.'

Blood pounded through her body, the thunder in her ears deafening as she gazed back, his touch sending erotic shocks through her body. She was drowning in the smoky grey of his eyes, her own will lost as she could only stare in stunned awareness of his maleness.

He moved first, bringing up a handful of colourful tops and skirts.

'Try these.' He tossed them over the mirror. 'This will go good with the suit.' He thrust a loose white cover-up into her hand. Lace traced the edges, ribbons tied it closed.

Anxious to cover her body from this disturbing man, Molly put it on. It was frilly, frivolous and feminine. She loved it.

'It's pretty. You look pretty, soft, feminine.' His voice was low, charming, sexy.

Her eyes flew to his, startled to find them narrowed as he looked at her. She could feel the pull of attraction from him as if he'd reached out and touched her. She couldn't look away. She had to, or she would be lost. But she couldn't move.

Since she'd grown she'd striven to always look cool and sophisticated and professional. Now this man, this stranger, had her all mixed up. All of her training and plans fled—for an instant she longed to be pretty, for him.

She'd taken off her glasses to try on the suit. He was slightly blurry in the mirror, but she was afraid to turn to face him—couldn't drag her eyes away from his, even to turn.

'This stuff must cost the earth,' she said stiffly, still caught in his gaze. She longed to purchase it, wear it for him, knowing it was a mistake.

'This is Mexico—nothing costs the earth here.' He smiled at her and reached up to undo her french braid. Molly couldn't move. She was mesmerised, staring at the two of them in the mirror as if she were watching two other people. Surely neither of them was her.

He spread her hair across her shoulders, trailing his fingers through its softness. With a sudden move, he scooped it up, exposing the delicate lines of her neck.

'You should get it cut,' he said again. 'Try on the other things. See what you want and we can go to the beach.'

'I can't.' Her disappointment caught her by surprise. 'I'm meeting my employer for lunch. I can't be late.'

'We can go for a while, if you hurry.' He let her hair slowly fall through his fingers and closed the curtain.

Molly tried the rest of the clothes on. All were delightfully feminine and pretty. If she could afford them, she would love to have them all. So much for planning to be prudent.

'Put your suit back on for the beach,' he called to her after ten minutes.

She complied, but pulled her white trousers and yellow top over. She was not yet ready to stroll the streets in only her swimsuit. She left the shirt open so the proprietor would not think she was trying to steal the suit. Pulling her hair back into a pony-tail, and firmly replacing her glasses, she looked more like herself. Taking a deep breath, she turned to leave.

When she pushed open the curtain, her companion smiled mockingly. 'How prim and proper.'

His gaze told her he knew why she was doing it. It had nothing to do with the others on the street. Only between themselves.

She flushed at his look, tilting her chin, wishing she could come back with a comment to set him in his place.

'I don't know if I want to go to the beach with you.'

It obviously missed setting him in his place. He ignored the comment and again took her arm, leading her to the cash register. Speaking rapidly in Spanish, he gestured to the clothes. The saleswoman took them and began wrapping them, all the while flirting with the man while she totalled the bill.

Molly watched, fascinated. The exchange went on for several minutes. Molly saw him smile at the woman, obviously not averse to using his charm to aid in the negotiations.

The saleswoman nodded, smiling broadly, and reached out a hand to shake his. He smiled deep into her eyes, holding her hand a shade longer than necessary, Molly noticed with a twinge. She cleared her throat.

Mocking eyes swung to her, and he told her the cost of the goods, watching her as she pulled out the money to pay for the clothes.

'They're so cheap,' she murmured as she counted the unfamiliar currency.

'Your *amigo*, he bargain good,' the woman said, smiling again at the man.

Molly looked up at him in surprise. 'Can you do that?'

He chuckled at her expression. 'It's expected. Never pay the asking price.'

Molly gathered her packages and moved towards the pavement, unsure just what to do. Would he expect her to go with him to the beach? She wanted to, yet was afraid. She didn't know this man at all.

'Where did you learn to speak Spanish so well?'

'Grew up in Texas, have lots of friends on both sides of the border.'

'Still live there?' she asked, her eyes carefully ahead. She wanted to know more about this man, but would he think her forward for asking?

He paused a moment. Did he not want to talk about himself? Was this just an attempt to pick up a girl, but nothing further? She looked at him, but he was watching the traffic. It was hectic as the cars barrelled along, uncaring of the pedestrians who tried to cross to the beach.

'Come on, we'll go to the beach as soon as we find a break in the traffic. Yes, I still live there.'

At a pause, he guided her through the standing cars until they reached the other side, and the sparkling white sand.

He looked down at her. 'And where do you live?'

'I live in Los Angeles.' Disappointment touched her. He didn't live anywhere near her. Once her visit here was over, she'd never see him again. The thought brought her up suddenly. She wasn't sure she'd even see him after today.

'What do you do?' she asked.

'I'm a cowboy.' He smiled a lazy smile at her, his eyes amused as they watched her expression.

For another moment, she was disappointed. She didn't know much about cowboys, but she knew they were never rich. And if she became involved with anyone she wanted him to have money. Not be *rich*, necessarily, just comfortably off so money would never be a worry. Though she doubted this man let anything worry him.

Good grief, she wasn't getting involved with this man. She'd just run into him on the street, spoken with him briefly last night.

'Wish I knew what you're thinking. Your expressions are fascinating.' His voice broke into her thoughts.

'I don't even know your name,' she said in surprise.

'Tell Hardin, Molly Spencer.'

'How did you know mine?' Had she told him last night?

He grinned and took her bags. 'Come on, the sand and sea are waiting and your time is short.'

They were scores of sun-worshippers already sprawled on the soft white sand. Scattered the length of the beach were conical thatched umbrellas offering spots of shade on the hot, sunny day. The water of the large bay was a deep blue, the small surface waves danced in the sunlight, reflecting the sun's rays like a million diamonds. The sky was a light blue, clear and limitless. On the opposite side of the bay she could see her hotel.

Molly shrugged out of her shirt and trousers and sat on the warm sand. The air was slightly salty, clean and fresh, blowing lightly in from the sea.

'This is great, so pretty and relaxing.'

'It's why people came to Acapulco,' he murmured, lying back on the sand, closing his eyes.

Molly studied him as he lay in the sun, his body big next to hers. He was relaxed against the white sand, his shoulders broad and muscular, his chest rising and falling slowly as he breathed. The mat of dark hair tapered to his flat stomach, the shorts fitted snugly, but no superfluous flesh bulged over the waist.

She looked at his face, his chin firm, his nose strong, his eyebrows dark and arched. The lashes lay on his cheeks, dark and thick. How unfair, she thought, that someone as masculine as he should have such beautiful lashes. She eyed him speculatively.

Molly took a deep breath and looked away, confused by the sudden desire to feel his warm skin beneath her fingers. She clenched her fists, trying to dispel the tingling yearning in her hands. Was she getting sunstroke?

Thinking would drive her crazy. She'd do better to get her mind away from his body. The tight shorts he wore were almost improper; at least they led her thoughts to the improper.

'Are you on vacation?' she asked desperately.

'Yep.'

'Staying at Las Casitas D'Oro?'

He opened one eye and looked over to her. 'Nope. That's for rich people.'

'Where are you staying?'

'Camping out.'

Was he too poor to even afford a room at one of the cheaper places? Molly wondered, dismayed.

'How did you get here?' she asked.

He rocked up on one elbow and looked up at her, his eyes narrowing against the sun's brightness.

'What is this, twenty questions?'

'I was just curious about you, that's all.'

'Good. Next you'll want to know if I'm married.'

A sudden panic gripped her. 'Are you?'

He shook his head, that heart-stopping lazy grin back on his face. 'Are you?'

'No.' She looked out over the water. There had never been anyone in her life. She hadn't had time for anyone. She had her own way to make, her own future to watch out for, and no time for meeting men and maybe falling in love. Once she felt secure in her career, once she had money in the bank, a safety net, then she'd see about finding someone to love, someone to share her life with. But not yet.

Tell reached out a finger and traced it from her shoulder down her arm to her wrist.

Molly shivered beneath his touch, her nerve-endings danced beneath his finger, yearned for more. She was unbearably conscious of his body only inches from hers, more aware of his body than any before, his broad shoulders, muscular chest, long legs. The hot sun beat on her shoulders and her legs, but the trail his finger left rivalled its heat. Her heart skipped faster, her breathing became constricted.

'Want to go to dinner with me tonight?' His voice was low and even.

'I don't know. Unlike you, I'm not here on vacation. I'm working.'

'Doing?'

'Secretary to a writer. I'm going to type her manuscript, organise notes, help with research. I'm new at it, so don't know yet what my schedule will be.'

'You must get some free time.'

'Yes, but I don't know when yet.'

'If you can go to dinner, call Miguel at the concierge's desk at your hotel—he'll be able to contact me. Just let me know.'

'OK,' she said shyly, hoping she had the time free, yet wondering if she'd be doing the right thing. She had just met him. While she was entranced by this man, and wouldn't mind spending some of her free time with him while in Acapulco, work came first.

She glanced at her watch, startled to see how late it was. 'I have to be going. I'm supposed to meet my boss at one.'

'Do you like your job?' he asked as she brushed off the sand before donning her street clothes.

'I like it so far. Beverley Sampson is my boss—have you heard of her?'

Tell nodded, rising to stand beside her, towering over her. The casual way he had about him had her wishing she was more comfortable with her own sexuality, wishing she could carry it off as effortlessly as he did. It took all her will-power to keep from looking at him, from feasting her eyes on the sensuality of his strong body.

He didn't speak as they walked back, and Molly began to wonder if he'd changed his mind about dinner. When she saw Beverley waiting at the edge of the car park, she pointed her out to Tell.

'That's Beverley there, my boss.'

He paused, turning partly away from Beverley, and handing Molly her bags.

'Remember, let Miguel know if you can go.'

'I will.' She didn't want to leave. She wanted to stay with him, forget her job, forget why she was in Acapulco. Appalled at where her thoughts were leading, she smiled shyly and turned towards her employer, hurrying to meet her. She remembered what Beverley had said about punctuality.

'Stay away from the likes of him,' Beverley said when Molly drew near. 'That riff-raff is not for the likes of you.'

'Do you know him?' Molly asked, surprised by her employer's outburst.

'Yes—trouble from the day he was born. What did you buy?'

Molly showed her the clothes in the bag, explaining as they walked to one of the open restaurants lining the beach. It was crowded inside, but Beverley was able to get a choice table. Seated on the seaward side, overlooking the beach and water, Beverley ordered seafood and Molly followed her employer's lead, wishing the whole while that it was the tall Texan opposite her.

CHAPTER THREE

LUNCH was pleasant on the shaded veranda over-looking the wide sandy beach. No more was said of Tell Hardin, though dozens of questions trembled on Molly's lips. Did Beverley know Tell personally, or was he known here in Acapulco only? What was his reputation? And what kind of trouble had he been since the day he was born?

Molly didn't feel comfortable enough with her new boss to enquire, but she longed to know the answers. Could she ask Tell herself?

Molly had only been with Beverley for two weeks. When Beverley had searched for a replacement for her newly married secretary, she had emphasised her practice of travelling and working in foreign countries, cautioning Molly that they could be gone for months at a time.

'That way I can satisfy my desire to travel, yet still keep working on current projects. Sometimes I combine working on one project with research on another. How does working in foreign places sound to you?'

'Wonderful!' Molly had replied quite truthfully. She had never been outside Los Angeles in all her twenty-four years. To travel to Acapulco within a few days of starting work seemed like a dream come true.

She had been delighted with Beverley's job offer. The writer paid top wages to compensate for the inconvenience of travelling. Molly, who thought travelling was wonderful, couldn't believe her good fortune at top wages to boot! Carefully planning to save a good portion, for she never knew how long a job would last, she still had quite enough for her modest needs.

As she ate, listening with half an ear to Beverley's chatter, she saw the dancing grey eyes of Tell. Regretfully she pushed his image aside. Not for her a cowboy unable to afford even a hotel room. Not for her the sexy, smoky grey eyes, narrowed in assessment as he studied her firm body in her bright bikini. At the remembrance, her skin flushed slightly and her heartbeat sped up. The lazy way he'd run his finger down her arm at the beach caused her to gaze out over the white sands, searching for his bronzed body, looking at all the tall male forms walking, or lounging on the sand.

No matter how hard she tried, she couldn't erase his image: it hovered before her, tantalising her, tormenting her. She longed to forget she had ever met him, longed for the excitement of her new job to consume her, not the unbidden thoughts of the tall, rugged male that wouldn't be banished.

He was riff-raff, trouble since he was born. She lightly licked her lips, wondering what kind of trouble he was, besides a decided threat to her own sanity.

Beverley began work in earnest when they returned to their rooms. Dictating passages, requesting verification of quotes and sources, she paced her large bedroom as she reeled off names, dates and events into her tape recorder. Molly's fingers flew as she captured the words on paper, transcribing as fast as she could type, knowing she would fall behind Beverley's rate of dictation.

The sun had set when Beverley called a halt to the activities.

'Finish that tape and this one in the morning. I'll check some of the other sources before continuing, so you should be able to catch up to me. Priscilla, my secretary before you, always was behind until the last day. You seem to type faster than she did, but I'll need to see your copy to know if you're as good as she was in the accuracy department.'

'I can finish up tonight,' Molly said quietly. The dinner hour was long past. She kept her eyes on Beverley, refusing to remember she'd been asked out, refusing to think of what might have happened if she'd been able to meet Tell for dinner, if they had been alone, the two of them.

'No, no, no. Order something in and enjoy the evening on the patio. You might want to swim; the water will be warm after today's heat. I'm going to take a hot bath and read. It's relaxing for me. I'll put on the air-conditioner and shut all the windows and be all by myself. You'll be all right on your own, won't you? See you after breakfast.' Beverley smiled and shooed her secretary from her room, drawing closed the sliding door and pulling her curtains.

Molly ordered a light salad and switched off her light, wandering out into the balmy night. The sparkling lights of Acapulco surrounded the bay, reflecting on the calm sea, a thousand lights to rival the stars in the clear night sky. The air was warm, scented with the sweet fragrance of night-blooming jasmine. It caressed her skin like a lover's touch. She smiled in quiet happiness.

'No dinner, huh?' Tell's silky voice spoke softly from the far corner. Surprised, Molly swivelled towards him, straining to see him in the dim light.

She darted a nervous glance at Beverley's room, relieved to see the curtains still drawn.

'What are you doing here?' Molly whispered, moving slowly over to where he sat stretched out on one of the pool's loungers.

'When you didn't call Miguel, I decided to come see why not. I saw. You were busy working. So I waited.'

'You shouldn't be here.' Her voice was low—she didn't want Beverley coming to investigate, didn't want her finding Tell here after warning her against him.

Tell ignored her and stood up slowly, peering down at her in the dark.

'So, have you eaten?'

'I ordered dinner in. They said it'd be about forty-five minutes.'

'Time for a swim, then. Do you still have your swimsuit on beneath those things?'

'Yes, but I don't think——'

Molly's voice stopped abruptly when Tell reached out and began unbuttoning her blouse. His fingers were warm as they brushed lightly against her skin, his eyes intent on the task. Slowly he pushed each button through its hole and the soft yellow cotton spread away from her, exposing the bright pink bikini.

She swallowed hard, mesmerised by his actions. She should stop him, protest, but she felt drugged, unable to move, unable to breathe. She could only look at Tell in the dim light, and tremble inside as his fingers brushed against her heated skin.

Slowly he opened her shirt and gently pushed it off her shoulders. Molly's insides began to melt, and her knees grew decidedly weak. She'd never had a man undress her before—it wreaked havoc with her senses. Tell's strong chest was before her, tantalising her with the mat of dark hair she longed to tangle her fingers in. She swallowed hard, tried to move her eyes from the enticing expanse.

When his fingers reached her waistband, slipping inside to work the fasteners, she felt her stomach muscles contract sharply, painfully. She tried to breathe, but couldn't. She stepped back, her hands pulling his free.

'I can manage,' she said huskily, turning slightly away, forcing her numb fingers to move. She stepped from her trousers, glad for the darkness. She was extremely conscious of how much of her was revealed by the daring bikini.

Tell kicked off his shorts, revealing a tight black swimsuit. It moulded him like a second skin and Molly had trouble keeping her eyes above his waist. He had a beautifully shaped body, wide shoulders, long legs and flat stomach. She could stare at him for hours.

Tell dived cleanly into the water, surfacing at the far edge. 'It's great.'

Molly placed her glasses on the table by the pool, flung old cautions to the wind and followed. When she broke the surface, she felt alive and awake as never before. The water was warm and silky against her skin, refreshing after the heat of the day and the hours spent over the computer.

'It is great! I can't believe I'm here.' She smiled, dragging her hair back.

'Not everyone has their own private pool,' Tell said whimsically.

They swam for a while, lazily back and forth in the warm water, the only light cast by the stars and the reflections from the far distant hotels.

When Molly had had enough, she swam to the stairs and slowly climbed from the water. The night air was only a few degrees cooler and caressed her skin like a lover. It dried her as she walked to the railing to enjoy the view. Wringing her hair, she left it hanging down her back, a damp cloak against her cooled skin.

Tell left the pool and joined her, in his hands hibiscus blossoms from the side of pool. Carefully he tucked a red one behind her ear; the pale pink one he gently tucked in the valley between her breasts.

Molly looked up, startled, her heart beating heavily at his touch. She'd never been touched so much by a man, moreover one she scarcely knew. It was unsettling, exciting and disturbing.

'Beverley said I shouldn't associate with you,' she blurted out.

He raised one eyebrow, his face amused. 'Oh, why's that?'

Molly wished she'd not spoken. She shrugged.

He reached for her arms, his fingers holding her firmly as he looked down at her, his thumbs moving against the soft satin of her inner arm. 'Why?'

'She said you were riff-raff, to stay away from you. That you were trouble since the day you were born.'

'Now how would she know that?' he asked softly, a look of pure amusement on his face.

'Probably recognised your type,' she snapped, tired of him laughing at her all the time. Couldn't he ever take her seriously?

'And what is my type, darlin'?' His voice was dangerously low, very calm. But Molly was warned by it.

'I don't know. Are you trouble?'

'No.'

He let her go and moved to lean against the railing, the twinkling lights of Acapulco behind him. Molly's eyes were used to the dim light surrounding them; she could see, though everything was blurry. She didn't want to put on her glasses. She didn't need them tonight.

As she stepped closer, she realised she was already dry, except for her hair. The hot night air had quickly absorbed the moisture. She felt cool, refreshed.

'Tell, I don't want to jeopardise this job. It's very important to me.'

'And seeing me would jeopardise it?' he asked.

'I don't know. Beverley was pretty specific.'

'She may dictate what you do during working hours, but your free time is surely your own?'

'Ordinarily, yes, but she's already said I shouldn't associate with you—what if she fires me?'

'Don't tell her.' There was a thread of amusement in his tone, and a hint of steel.

Molly hesitated, thinking what that would entail, wondering if she wanted to do that. She'd always been straightforward; to go behind Beverley's back and against her wishes seemed somehow distasteful.

Yet there was no denying her feelings. She was drawn to Tell Hardin. She liked being around him, though he overwhelmed her. Surely there'd be no harm in spending some of her free time with him? Just to see some of the sights of Acapulco with him. He had offered. She wouldn't neglect her work in any way.

And she knew better than to fall for him. He was charming and sexy and much too smooth and knowing for her to handle. But surely it could do no harm to spend a few hours in his company?

And be the envy of all the women in town. The thought sprang unbidden to mind. She smiled a little at that. She would be the envy of all who saw them. Tell was sexy as hell.

'Molly, think of the fun we could have here. I've been here before. I can show you the cliff-divers of La Quebrada, we can see the underwater shrine of the Virgin of Guadalupe, go snorkelling, try the parachute rides, or the moonlight cruises of the bay. We can bargain at the markets and ride horses on the beaches. What do you say?'

She smiled at the pictures his words painted. It sounded exciting, exotic . . . and expensive. She came back to reality with a bang.

'It sounds wonderful but very expensive. Just who's footing the bill for all this—me? Maybe that's what Beverley meant,' she said evenly. That would explain why a man as good-looking as Tell would spend time with her, instead of picking up some of the more beautiful girls who filled the beaches.

'Now I've heard everything. What do you think, I'm some damned gigolo?' He stood up abruptly and took a threatening step towards her.

'I don't know the first thing about you! You show up bringing towels. Why? To check out the new arrivals, see if one is an impressionable American girl to sweep off her feet with your charm and your damned good looks? Take her everywhere, but enjoy yourself, too, at her expense?'

'No one said you had to pay my way.' His voice was hard, his stance taut, threatening.

'Oh, I suppose cowboys have lots and lots of money and camp out when they come to Acapulco just for the fun of it!'

'What do you do, ask to see a man's bank balance before going out with him? If it meets your standards fine, if not, forget it? You're no better than a trashy gold-digger. I wish you joy of your stay here!'

He snatched up his shorts and stalked to the gate, vaulting over it to melt into the inky dark shadows of the hill. In seconds he disappeared, without a sound.

'Tell!' Molly took a step towards the wall. She didn't want him to leave, especially not this way.

Even as she started after his departing figure, the knocker sounded on her door. Dinner had arrived. With a long look of regret at the dark hillside, she turned and quickly crossed the patio to her room.

She took the hibiscus from between her breasts, dropping it on the dresser as she passed. She shouldn't have been so outspoken. She didn't really think he was a gigolo, did she?

The question played over and over as she ate, showered and prepared for bed. Searching the empty patio one last time, she turned off her light and went to sleep. Tell had not returned. She hadn't expected him to, only wished that he would.

She should not have said all she had to him, but it was said partly from fear. Fear she'd grow to like him, fear of what he would demand from her. Life had been muddled and disruptive in her younger days, and Molly fought for stability now. She liked things done in a proper and orderly fashion. She couldn't afford to let some drifting cowboy turn her world upside-down for a few weeks while he holidayed, then pass on. She just couldn't.

But had he already done so?

The light from the sun was full on the patio when Molly awoke the next morning. She dressed in her new white shorts and a striped red and blue top Tell had picked out. She wondered if he would see her wearing them. The top was short, exposing her midriff, and she liked the feel of the warm, moist tropical air against her skin. Her hair tied up off her neck, she wandered out to the patio. Spotting her glasses where she'd left them last night, she slipped them on and sank into the chair to eat breakfast.

Beverley was not yet awake, or at least had not opened her curtains, and Molly felt free to enjoy the quiet morning air. The sun softly kissed her skin and she shifted her position to take full advantage of it. She wanted to get a tan so that she looked healthy. Against the others on the beach yesterday, she'd looked positively pale.

Without conscious thought, she let her eyes scan the hillside. Where was Tell? Was his camp near by? He'd never said. Somehow she thought it closer to town, but then how did he get here? Their *casita* was one of the uppermost in the complex. There were only two higher than theirs. Terraced below them were dozens more, each with its own patio, pool and spectacular view of Acapulco.

Breakfast finished, Molly was impatient to get started on her work. Maybe she'd suggest to Beverley that she take the computer into her room. She'd be able to work whether Beverley wanted to or not. She looked out to the deep blue of the bay and remembered the sparkling beach.

She'd better get to work; that would be better than sitting alone with her own thoughts.

Closing her eyes and leaning back in her chair didn't help. She only saw Tell's face. Shifting her position, she remembered him in the shop yesterday, and the first night she'd met him. Opening her eyes, she was disgusted with herself for thinking so much about him. He was just a man she'd met a couple of times. Granted, the most exciting and sexy man she'd ever seen, but she needed to forget him! She'd known all along he was not for her.

Beverley kept a frantic pace for two days. Once she'd flashed open her curtains and slid her door open, she had been hard to keep up with. She approved Molly's idea of moving the computer, but was forever wandering back and forth between the two rooms. She kept a recorder going day and evening, words pouring forth, ideas and scenes that had to be captured. Molly wondered whether she could keep up the pace.

Fingers flying, Molly sped each day to keep pace with her new boss. She improved her typing, and was able to deliver clean copy of the steady stream of words Beverley dictated each day. Molly found herself growing more and more interested in the life and times of General Black Jack Pershing, the subject of Beverley's biography.

From time to time, however, mocking grey eyes danced before her own. She would lose track of Beverley's words and hear over and over the accusation Tell made. It hurt that he thought she was a gold-digger. The thought burned into her. How dared he? Then shamefacedly she'd remember she had accused him of being a gigolo. Which was worse?

Each night she stayed out on the patio until late, hoping he would come again and talk to her. She had never been so caught up with another person before, so drawn to a man. She wanted to tell him of the work she was doing, hear what he was doing, hear about his life in the States, share some of the sights of Acapulco as he had suggested.

But each night she sat alone. The beauty of the warm Mexican nights mocked her single status, the romance of old Mexico a fairy-tale to be dreamed of, but not experienced. She was lonely, a loneliness never before experienced. Was it the sweet scent of the evening air, the loveliness of the tropical night sky, or the beauty and romance that was Acapulco which emphasised her solitary state? Or was it the memory of the few meetings she'd had with a romantic fantasy man, the way he'd made her feel so alive, so conscious of everything around her, from the beauty of the Mexican countryside to the loveliness of the blue waters and white sands of the bay? So conscious of her own body and the emotions and longings he awakened within her.

The next afternoon, Beverley stopped work early, just after lunch.

'I want to lie in the sun, get some tan. I know it dries your skin, but, at my age, who cares?'

'I just have one more tape to complete,' Molly murmured as she smiled up at the older woman.

'You can finish that up this afternoon. Run down to the gift shop for me. The kind of suntan lotion I like is carried by the hotel and I'm out. I want to put some on to help conserve what little moisture I have left. Also, see if they have any fashion magazines. I always like to look at the fashions of the different countries when I visit. They can be so different from what we see in the States. Not that what we see in Los Angeles is representative of the whole US, mind you. The outlandish outfits I see sometimes positively make me want to laugh out loud.'

Her voice trailed off as she walked back to her room. Presumably to change, Molly thought, smiling as she attacked the last tape. She had been lucky to get the job with Beverley. She was easy to work for, made few demands and had plenty to say. But she rarely stopped talking.

Reaching a quitting point, Molly was glad for the exercise walking down to the hotel gift shop would afford. She would finish the last half of the tape later.

Since Las Casitas D'Oro was built on a hillside, the incline was steep. The roadway for the hotel was not wide, and as she walked along the edge she kept a wary eye out for one of the hotel jeeps. She wondered if all drivers were like Beverley when they got behind the wheel of a jeep. They hurled around corners as if they owned the road and she didn't want to be hit by one.

The gift shop and lobby were together just inside the mighty stone pillars that marked the entrance. Passing the concierge desk, Molly paused, glancing at the man behind the ornate wooden desk. She slowed her pace as she thoughtfully entered the gift shop. Was that Miguel? Would he know where Tell was?

She looked for the items her employer had requested, charging them to their rooms. As she idly studied the other magazines, her heartbeat began to pick up as she considered talking to Miguel. Ask him about Tell. Dared she? Would he know who she was,

know of the last conversation she'd had with Tell?
The accusations they'd thrown at each other?

Did he know where to find Tell, how to reach him?
Or had that been just for that one day? Had Tell
stayed within calling distance that one day, in case she
could go to dinner?

It really was not the proper thing for a woman to
ask after a man—though this was the nineties. But
Molly had never done such a thing. Yet surely just to
ask after him would be OK.

Heart pounding, stomach full of butterflies, Molly
approached the desk. The young Mexican looked up
and smiled at her, his eyes dark and liquid in his clean-
shaven face.

'Excuse me, are you Miguel?' Molly asked.

'*Sí, señorita*. How may I be of assistance to you?'
The smooth rhythm of the Mexican accent was
pleasant to her ear.

'I wondered if you know Tell Hardin? Know where
I could reach him?'

'Señor Hardin is not staying at the hotel.'

'I know. I just ... one time he said I could leave a
message with you to give to him. I wondered if I still
could?'

'And the message?'

Molly stared at the man, her mind blank. What kind
of message could she give? Come see me? After what
she'd said? Her face fell. It was stupid to bother the
concierge.

'I guess I don't have a message after all.'
Dispiritedly, she turned away. How did you leave a
message for a man whom you had insulted and sent

away? And called vile names. She was better off forgetting him.

Only it was so much easier to say than to do.

CHAPTER FOUR

KNOWING the angry accusations she'd made were the reasons Tell hadn't come around again, Molly had no one to blame but herself. How could she have blurted out such a thing? She sighed as she made the long climb back to their *casita*. She wished she could relive those few moments—she would have said it differently.

Joining Beverley on the patio, she gave her the sunscreen. Leaving her for her swim, Molly went back inside to finish the last side of the tape.

Molly enjoyed the work; the information Beverley imparted was informative and entertaining. Though that lady talked a blue streak, her writing was succinct and enlightening. Molly wondered at the dichotomy.

Frowning, Molly also wondered how long it would be before she stopped seeing Tell between her and the computer screen. Blinking her eyes only brought his image in better focus. She had not forgotten a single thing about him, from the way his skin crinkled slightly at his eyes when he smiled to the lips she'd longed to feel against her skin.

She shook her head. She had to finish the tapes. She didn't want Beverley to find any fault with her work. This job was too important to her, the security it represented too precious to jeopardise by inattention.

When she finished it was almost dinnertime. She sat back in her chair and gazed out over the pool, out beyond to the blue waters of the bay. Only three nights ago she'd had an offer for dinner. She wished she had been able to take Tell up on his offer. Where would that have led them? To the same angry words they'd sparred with on the patio? Or to different topics, different moods?

Was he or wasn't he a gigolo? He'd asked her out, not saying anything about her paying. Sighing, Molly closed her eyes. She should have had more information before accusing him. He'd suggested places to go, things to do and she'd immediately jumped to the conclusion he wanted her to treat. Why?

Was it because she couldn't believe an exciting man like Tell would want her company without something in return from her? She led a quiet life, struggling to make ends meet, no time for frivolous games. She knew so little about men in general and Tell specifically, aside from his pure animal magnetism. How awful if she'd misjudged him.

Opening her eyes, she turned off the computer and called for room service. Another night alone in paradise. Maybe she should change her clothes and go to one of the discos in town. There'd be crowds of happy people, joyful music, and plenty of activity to entertain her.

She shrank away from the thought. She was too shy to venture forth on her own. Too 'prim and proper'. Darn it, was everything to remind her of Tell Hardin? She'd only met the man a couple of times. Why had he made such an impression on her?

Molly had an early night, eager for the morning and the work that Beverley was sure to produce. She needed the fast-paced activity to take her mind off the turmoil of her thoughts.

To her surprise and disappointment, Beverley was not in the mood to write the next morning.

'I get like this sometimes,' she said brightly, not at all deterred by her block. 'I just pour myself into pages and pages, then can't do anything for a couple of days. I guess I have to recharge my batteries. I'll just lie in the sun, or go shopping or call up some of my friends who live here. I'll be back on track either tomorrow or the next day. Don't worry about it. The only thing is, I never know when I'll be busy and when I won't. Take your free time now, because I might want to work non-stop for the next ten days.'

'Isn't there something I can do to help?' Molly asked, thinking of research, or editing. There must be something she could do to keep herself busy.

'No, nothing. I don't even want to think about it, though I'm probably thinking about it in my subconscious even as we speak. But that's not my *conscious*, so I don't know I'm thinking about it. But no, nothing now. It will all come clear in another day or two. You go off and enjoy yourself.'

Molly looked dismayed. Last night had been bad enough, long and endless and boring. What would she do with the whole day?

'Take the jeep. I'll call friends. If I want to go anywhere, they can take me,' Beverley said, pouring the last of the coffee into her cup.

'I really don't have any place to go,' Molly said.

'Nonsense. If there is no place special you want to see, try the hotel's beach club. It has a couple of sheltered saltwater pools with tropical fish and plant life, or you can swim in the bay itself. They have a grand buffet there; you can have lunch and enjoy yourself. Don't give a thought to me. I'll be fine. Just fine.'

Beverley again reminded Molly of a bright, sprightly bird. She hid her smile.

'OK, maybe I'll try it.'

Hanging around as long as she dared, to make sure Beverley didn't change her mind, Molly nevertheless started for the beach club by the late morning. She'd swim, eat lunch at the buffet and see what else there was to do. Maybe she'd venture into the city later, though she rather doubted she'd feel brave enough to go alone.

She stopped in at the lobby, asking Miguel for directions to the beach club. Since Las Casitas D'Oro was situated high on a mountainside overlooking the bay, the drive to the beach was lengthy. She would pass through some of the expensive residential sections of Acapulco before arriving at the private beach club of the hotel.

Confident she knew where she was going, she started off slowly, still nervous in the open jeep. Though she felt she was much more cautious than Beverley had been, she was still fearful with the lack of roof and doors.

Crossing the highway, she started down the hill. Tall palms and colourful oleander and hibiscus lined the road. Behind stone walls she could catch glimpses of the large villas built with their backs to the road, facing the view of the city, and the beautiful bay.

Stopping at one intersection, Molly was startled when a brown body came out of the shadows of the oleander and calmly slid into the seat next to her. His movements were smooth, like a sleek wolf on the prowl.

Molly's heart-rate increased as she recognised Tell Hardin. She became instantly aware of the brightness of the day, the rich tones of the red hibiscus and pink oleander lining the road. Despite the unfriendly words they'd exchanged, happiness welled within her at the sight of him.

'What are you doing here?' Not the most auspicious greeting. She flushed and bit her lip. He'd never guess how glad she was to see him. She had thought she never would again.

He lifted his lips in a lazy smile and ran his eyes down her figure. She had worn her bikini under the frilly, lacy cover-up. Her legs were beginning to tan and were shapely beneath the edge of the cover-up.

'You look good enough to eat,' he drawled. 'Where are you heading?'

She was flustered under his gaze and turned back to the road, easing across the intersection and starting down again.

'I'm going to the hotel's beach club,' she told him.

'Nice place. We can go snorkelling there.'

She threw him a dark glance. 'It's for guests only,' she said.

'You're a guest. I'm your guest. We're both guests.'

She bit her lip in indecision. The dark thoughts from the previous night reared their heads. Did he want to spend time with her, or was he using her only as a means to enjoy his holiday in places he wouldn't ordinarily be permitted to enter? She darted a swift glance, the indecision clearly written on her face. He didn't look as if he depended on a woman for anything.

'Tell, I don't think . . .'

'Good, don't. Did you miss me?'

Strong and rugged, he displayed an arrogant, don't-give-a-damn attitude that exuded confidence and assurance. The few times she'd been around him he'd taken charge, deftly, swiftly, totally. It didn't look as if today was any different.

She swallowed hard, not wanting to admit she'd missed him. Did nothing ever bother him?

'The truth now,' he warned her, his tone full of amusement.

'Well, I did notice you weren't trespassing as much lately,' she said, her eyes carefully on the narrow street.

He chuckled and drew a warm finger along her leg. Molly caught her breath, almost losing control of the car, almost losing control of herself. His touch was like an electric shock, sending delightful waves of pulsating pleasure through her whole body.

'Thought your boss would be working you so hard you'd not even notice.'

'I have today off,' she said shyly, achingly aware of his brown body just inches from her. He was wearing his cut-offs again, and scruffy sandals. His muscles slid easily beneath the taut skin and seeing his every move from the corner of her eye made it very difficult to concentrate on her driving.

Her body was aware of his proximity, her leg craving further touches from his fingers. Her breathing became more laborious. She gripped the wheel, forcing her mind to concentrate on her driving.

'Good, we'll spend it at the beach club. They have a good lunch.'

'Tell . . .'

'Unless you're spending the day with someone else.'

'No.'

'Good. Here we are, turn here.'

She came upon the gate sooner than she expected and had to turn sharply to enter. The attendant smiled, recognising the hotel's jeep, and waved her in. Molly couldn't believe how easy it was.

'Easy, if you know how,' Tell murmured as she pulled into the parking area.

'I don't think you should be here.' She bravely turned to him, not expecting the shock of desire that flooded through her when she faced him. His shoulders looked broader than she remembered, his chest solid and tantalising with its dark mat of hair and strong muscles that had her fingers aching to rub them. Did he ever wear a shirt? She raised her gaze to clash with his and couldn't look away. His eyes were quizzical in the morning light, silvery grey and sparkling. Faint lines radiated from the corners, lighter in colour than the rest of his skin. He must narrow his eyes against the sun. Did he look far distances when riding the ranges of Texas?

He reached up and withdrew her glasses. Molly blinked, but he was close enough to be in focus. She held her breath. What would come next?

'Do you have sunglasses?' he asked, his eyes dropping to her lips.

Molly licked them, her tongue flicking out quickly to wet them, withdrawing.

'Yes, in my hold-all.'

'Put them on, or you'll get wrinkles.' His gaze never left her lips and Molly dropped her own gaze to his mouth. Jerking her head away, she rummaged through her bag, finding the glasses and thankfully drawing them on. They would offer her some measure of protection.

Tell smiled and climbed from the jeep, waited for her to come around and then headed for the water.

There were two large saltwater pools, separated from the bay itself by huge stone walls. Beneath each wall was access to the bay—the water in the pools constantly changed with the ebb and flow of the sea. Colourful chairs and recliners lined both pools, umbrellas here and there to shelter the newcomers. There was a motorised bar that circulated around and to the far side Molly saw the tables and buffet set for lunch beneath the shade of a blue and white awning. Tall palms swayed in the breeze, colourful flowers banked the hill as it rose from the bay. It was a beautiful setting.

'You didn't bring a towel,' she said as she dropped her bag on one of the recliners.

'Don't need to; they provide them here.'

'You've been here before, haven't you?' He knew more about it than she did, and she'd read the brochure in the hotel room.

'Mmm, once or twice.'

Who with? she wondered.

'Want to swim, snorkel, or lie in the sun?' Tell surveyed the area and nodded to the small booth with snorkel gear.

'I'd like to try snorkelling. I've never done it.' Molly said, following his gaze.

Tell walked casually over and spent several moments talking with the young man on duty there. He gathered up the masks, snorkels and fins and rejoined Molly.

She sat on one of the chairs, watching the transaction from a distance, feasting her eyes on the tall Texan who had invaded her life so suddenly and completely invaded her senses. Who was he? Why had he singled her out for attention? He was almost too good to be true: rugged, handsome, confident.

Glancing around, she saw she was not the only woman watching Tell. Several others followed his half-clothed body as he moved easily around the edge of the tidal pool. For a moment happiness threatened to overwhelm Molly—he was coming back to *her*. She was almost smug in her feelings. He hadn't glanced at any of the tanned beauties displaying themselves to best advantage in the morning sun.

He dropped the equipment on an adjacent chair when he reached her, and pulled her to her feet. Before she could say anything, his hands moved to the ribbons holding her cover-up closed and slowly began to undo them. Drawing the moment out, he slowly pulled the first ribbon, the material falling open, then the second, and the third.

Tension rose in Molly until she could almost touch it. His eyes were intently watching the material fall open, watching as his fingers released the ribbons and slowly let the soft satin drift through his fingers before releasing it.

'You're always undressing me,' she said softly.

Molly closed her eyes, not believing she'd said the words aloud, she could feel the heat rise in her face. How could she blurt out something like that? Remembering how she felt the evening by the pool, she knew she should demand he stop. But she didn't want to.

When she opened her eyes and ventured to look at Tell, he was gazing down at her, his eyes no longer amused or mocking, but serious.

'One day,' he said softly, holding her gaze, 'I won't stop at the swimsuit either.'

He waited a moment then the familiar amusement crept back into his eyes.

'Relax and enjoy yourself. Acapulco is for sun, sea, sand and sex.'

Colour stained her cheeks. Had she given him the wrong impression? Did he think she went in for casual sex? Embarrassment flooded through her. She had to set him straight, right now. She took a deep breath. She couldn't let him think . . .

Tell chuckled, his teeth white in the deep tan of his face. Taking her chin in his fingers, he tilted her face up a little.

'Very prim and proper! I wish you could see the expressions chase across your face. OK, if sex is out, we'll have fun other ways.'

She frowned, perversely disappointed he wasn't more let down at her response. He was always laughing at her; why did he spend time with her, just because she afforded him such great amusement?

The warmth from his fingers spread throughout Molly's body. She felt deliciously weak and yet at the same time excited and keyed up. She looked into his eyes and felt herself drowning in a silvery sea of emotions never experienced before.

She wanted him to kiss her and as the thought took hold it was all Molly could do to keep herself from throwing herself into his arms.

Sex would be wonderful with Tell, she knew. Her heart began beating heavily at the thought. But she'd want more, want to make love, not just have the physical joining. Want him to look on her as special, not just another girl picked up in Acapulco.

'Now what are you thinking?' His voice was low, sexy, his thumb gently rubbing her chin, his eyes narrowed as he watched her. Molly's stomach lurched and she jerked her head free.

'Nothing.' Was that thready voice hers? She needed more resolution. She could so easily become devastated by this man; she had to resist.

'Let's go snorkelling.'

Tell helped her don the snorkels, face masks and fins and led Molly in the huge natural sea pool nearest their chairs. He showed her how to breathe, adjusted her flippers and dived cleanly into the water. Molly followed, knowing instantly she was not the swimmer he was.

But it didn't matter. He held back to stay with her and she marvelled at the beauty beneath the surface of the water. The small tropical fish that darted before her outstretched hands were colourful, wearing patterns of yellow and blue and red. The light sand was a perfect background for the lacy seaweed that grew near the rocks, and the small pink and rose sea anemones that waved their arms in the gently moving water. Molly was fascinated with the beauty of the setting and bubbling with happiness when Tell tapped her on her shoulder and motioned her upright.

She shook her head when she surfaced, drawing up the faceplate, flipping some of her hair back. It was in the way—maybe she *should* cut it.

'It's wonderful!' She smiled at him, her excitement evident in her face.

He smiled and nodded. 'I know, but we have to stop now. Your back will be blistered if we don't. The water draws the sun and you're lying on top too much with your fair skin.'

Knowing he made sense, she was still loath to stop. With one more reluctant look at the treasures beneath the surface, she slowly swam to the side. She wished she had the deep tan he had and wondered how he'd got so brown all over.

Tell was by the stone steps leading up to the patio, waiting for her. Trying to take off her flippers, Molly fell over, the water coming over her head, and she almost choked because of her laughter.

He hauled her up and held on to one arm, his laughter mingling with hers. She slipped off the flippers and reached up to take off the mask. The rubber strap was tangled in her hair.

'Ouch, I can't get it,' she groaned.

'Turn around; I can.'

She obediently turned in the chest-high water, swaying slightly in the movement of the gentle waves, her arms floating on the surface, lassitude and contentment spreading through her.

He pulled her hair a little, and tears flooded her eyes.

'Ouch!'

'Done.' He turned her around, seeing the tears glimmer in the sun.

Molly saw the spiky lashes of his eyes coming closer, until she closed her own.

His lips touched hers, cool and salty. He moved them against hers, drawing a response. Molly smiled and opened her eyes to see him drawing back slightly. She felt as if she were dreaming, floating on a soft sea of emotions. She closed her eyes again and he kissed her again, but this time it was not a peaceful, dreamy kiss, it was charged, fiery, electric, exhilarating. His lips were hot now, demanding, forceful.

Her own moved in response as her body suddenly clamoured for contact with him. She moved through the warm water up against his body, her arms encircling his neck and her lips moving feverishly against his. She sought to give whatever he demanded, moving to get closer, to feel the strength and warmth of his skin against her own, the crisp hair of his chest heightening her awareness.

His hands moved against her back, lower, to caress the small of her back just above her bikini. His fingers trailed electric shocks of pleasure along her spine, across the sensitised muscles of her back. She could not get close enough, moving her body against his as she tried to, her lips hot and responsive, moving against his, revelling in the feel of his mouth on hers, his hands bringing shimmering waves of delight, the strength of his chest, his legs against hers.

He drew back, breathing heavily in the bright morning sun. Molly felt as if her only support was gone, and slowly she let her hands drop from his shoulders, afraid to meet his look, self-consciousness weighing her down. Could she just sink in the water and never come up again?

He tilted her chin once more and dropped a light kiss on her lips.

'You should get your hair cut.'

She blinked, not expecting that.

'Why?'

'First, it's got to be hot in this climate, or in LA for that matter. Second, it wouldn't get tangled in snorkelling masks.'

She stepped back, not knowing whether to be angry or not. After the magic of his kiss, all he thought about was her hair.

'But the real reason you should get it cut,' he said softly, 'is that it would expose your pretty neck, the easier to reach.' Tell leaned over and kissed her softly on her neck, sweeping her damp tangled hair aside. Straightening, he smiled directly in her eyes.

Molly swallowed hard, her emotions on a roller-coaster. She was in over her head and didn't know what to do.

CHAPTER FIVE

MOLLY moved in a daze to the lounger where her towel lay. She dried off and sat back, putting her sunglasses firmly in place. It gave her some shelter from Tell's penetrating gaze.

He followed her back and lay down in the lounger beside her, pulling the chair close to hers. The even rise and fall of his chest soon let her know he'd fallen asleep in the sultry air.

Molly lay still, though her mind raced. She finally felt his kiss, felt his firm lips, knew what it was like to have his skin against hers. But it was his lips that claimed her attention, hot and passionate; the feelings he evoked burned in her memory, through her body. Did he kiss everyone like that, or only her? The tip of her tongue licked her top lip.

Her body suffused with heat as she relived those pulsating moments, she sat up, hoping for some cooling breeze to bring down her temperature. She might have to go back into the water, or at the very least change the direction of her thoughts.

'What's wrong?' Tell asked lazily from beside her.

She looked over. He hadn't even opened his eyes. How did he know anything was wrong?

'I'm hot,' she said, holding her breath, hoping he'd not ask her why.

'I know, it's hot as blazes out here. Hold on, I'll get us an umbrella.' His supple body rose effortlessly from the recliner and he moved easily across the hot patio. In only seconds he returned with a large umbrella that shaded both their chairs. Setting it up, he moved his chair closer to Molly's and sank back down, eyes closing.

'Thank you,' she murmured, turning slightly so she could watch him.

His lips turned up slightly, but he didn't open his eyes. 'Tell me what you've been doing,' he ordered.

Molly launched into an account of the work she'd been doing for Beverley, the long hours, how interesting it all was for her, keeping a wary eye on him, lest he grow bored with her talking.

'She's quite different from what I expected, but fascinating to work for.'

'Not worked for her for long, eh?'

'No, I just got the job. My old job was ending, and I thought I'd be out of work for a while, but I found this right away. It pays well and there's the extra bonus of travel. I never thought I'd come to Acapulco.'

'Nice perk. Tell me about LA.'

Molly sank back, closing her eyes, slowly telling Tell some of what her life was like, glossing over how alone she was, and how lonely sometimes. Briefly she mentioned that her parents were dead, but didn't tell him of the struggle it had been just to make ends meet when they had been alive. She didn't talk of how lacking in the basic security as a child had made her value security above all else. Instead she emphasised her progress in work, the reading and sewing she liked to do for relaxation.

Then she paused, not wanting to talk about herself—she knew about that. She wanted to learn more about Tell.

'What about you? What's it like being a cowboy?' she asked.

'Only thing I know. I like it. Riding most days, fooling with stupid cattle. But the range is open and free and I can do what I want, when I want. Don't have to answer to anyone. I'm outside all the time, which I like.'

She could imagine him on a tall horse, sitting proud in the saddle, and looking over the miles of open range that stretched out before him. She tried to imagine him in an office, or shop, but was unable to do so—he belonged to the outdoors.

'Want lunch? The buffet is good.'

Molly opened her eyes, a vague sense of unease troubling her. How did he know so much about this place?

'Sure.'

She donned her frilly white cover-up and they strolled over to the tables set up under the colourful awning. There was a slight breeze and with the shade from the sun it was pleasant for eating.

The buffet was long, with all sorts of salads and cold meats and cheeses, and with tall fruit punches and glasses of iced tea for beverages. Molly loaded her plate with the tropical fruit salads, wanting to eat the mangoes and passion fruit not readily found in the US. She was passing another offering, when Tell stopped her.

'Take some *ceviche*. You've never tried it, I bet.'

'No, what is it?'

'Take some and try it. It's a local speciality, I'll bet you love it.'

He scooped a portion on to her plate and a more generous one on his own.

Taking a glass of iced tea, Molly found a table near the water. A Mariachi band played softly in the background. She surveyed the view, the sparkling blue water, tall, stately palms swaying in the breeze, the cloudless sky, the circle of hills that enclosed Acapulco Bay. And the tall, dark man coming to sit across from her. Molly felt daring and reckless and slightly improper.

Lunch turned out to be more fun than she expected. Tell told her stories of Texas and experiences he'd had in his work with an amusing, mocking inflexion. She laughed at his tales, knowing they had to be exaggerated, but finding them entertaining and enlightening. When he asked her questions, she turned them away, giving away little about herself. She didn't have a happy childhood to remember and didn't want the dark memories she did have spoiling her happy day.

And it was happy. She felt reckless and free and all because of the way he looked at her, the way he spoke of things designed to make her laugh. Yet his eyes spoke of other things, which made her breathless at times, very aware of the man opposite her.

After they'd eaten, Molly was presented with the bill. She looked up into Tell's eyes, startled into remembering her accusation of the other evening. Dropping her eyes before his steely glint, she knew he remembered as well, and was angered anew. She signed the ticket, writing her room number down. She'd have to settle with Beverley later for Tell's lunch. Molly didn't expect her boss to foot that bill. She wondered how she would explain it to her boss. Time to think up something before then.

But some of the sparkle of the day dimmed for her. Was he only here for what he could get from her? To further enjoy his vacation at her expense? What if she hadn't let him come to the beach club—would he have wanted to take her somewhere else?

When she rose, he slipped beside her, his hand encircling her upper arm, his fingers gripping hard. Quickly he half marched her from the dining area, out into the brilliant, hot sunshine. Passing their chairs, he continued around the point of land, around the banks of oleander to the side facing the Pacific Ocean. There was no one else on this stretch of beach; the wind was stronger and the surf powerful.

'I'm not some damned gigolo, Miss Gold-digger. If it's so important to you, I can bring you the damned money for lunch tonight.' He jerked her in front of him, glaring down at her through narrowed slate-grey eyes.

She was frightened, his anger was so intense. She knew he had no money on him. His shorts and swimsuit were too revealing to permit even a folded peso in the pockets. Anyway, one meal among friends was nothing. If he continued to cadge off her, she could always say no. If she thought he was taking advantage of her.

But she didn't want him so angry.

'I don't want any money. I was enjoying the day, Tell. I'm glad you came with me.' Her voice was soft, shaky. She raised her eyes as high as his lips, they started to soften and she dared a glance up.

His head blotted out the sky and his mouth found hers in a hard, compelling kiss. His lips were hot and commanding, demanding a response Molly was only too eager to give. His hand slipped beneath her cover-

up and pulled her to his hard, warm body. His legs
spread to hold them both and the kiss deepened as he
moved urgently against her mouth, opening her lips
and plunging deep within the hot moisture.

Molly's world exploded with sensation and quivered
with passion. Her legs threatened to fail her, her arms
found themselves around his neck, holding on, pulling
him as close as he was moulding her. She couldn't
think, only feel, feel the wondrous excitement building
at his touch. The blood pounded in her head, blotting
out the muffled roar of the surf behind her. Her heart
raced, her breathing stopped.

Tell moved to trail fiery kisses along her cheek, nip
her earlobe, move down her throat, kissing the fluttering pulse at its base. Molly closed her eyes, caught
up in the physical delight his touch evoked. She felt
his hard body against her, and his arousal raised her
to new heights. She never wanted the moment to end.
Her own mouth was hot, unsatiated, her skin on fire
for his touch, and the roughness of his hands only
intensified the fiery delight.

But, sanity said, it had to end. They were on a
public beach, where anyone could wander by at any
time. Reluctantly, she opened her eyes, dazzled in the
bright sunlight, her nerve-endings quivering in aroused
passion, longing for more, much more. She was
shocked at her own response to him.

'Tell . . .' she said softly, imprinting the feel of his
hot lips on her throat for all time, memorising the feel
of his muscles beneath her fingers, the strength of his
shoulders and the tantalising feel of the crisp hair on
his strong chest. These she would always remember—
her fingers were reluctant to leave, she was reluctant
to stop, but they must!

'Tell . . . please, we should stop.'

'Why?' He looked down at her eyes, his molten steel, smouldering and passion-drugged. Flicking to her mouth and back to her eyes, he asked again, 'Why, Molly, don't you like it?'

'Yes. I do.' She struggled to stand away from him, before she lost all sense of decorum. 'Too much. Tell, we're on a public beach!'

He smiled at her, the passion gradually fading to be replaced with the familiar amusement. 'And Miss Prim and Proper finds that appalling, does she?'

'Well, I think we should——'

'What we should do is go back to my camp where there is no one around for miles and make long, slow, passionate love. While the afternoon away and sleep together tonight.'

Colour stained her cheeks and she pushed against his shoulders.

'I can't do that,' she whispered.

He let her slip back, his hands coming to rest on her ribs, his thumbs beneath her breasts. 'No, I don't think you could.' He sighed.

Molly looked over his left shoulder, across the white sands of the beach. Because of the heavy surf, it was not used by the sun-and-sea-loving crowd. But someone could venture for a walk.

'Come on, there's some hammocks over yonder. We can rest after our lunch, go swimming later.' Tell slowly let his hands slide down her body, slip out from beneath her frilly cover-up. Taking one of her hands in his, he started briskly across the sand to the large hammocks spread beneath a thatched awning. Sheltered from the hot sun, open to the breeze and the view of the Pacific, it was an ideal spot for a nap.

Tell sat at the edge of the first hammock, and turned Molly around so that she faced him. With a lazy smile, he slipped his hands back up beneath her cover-up, along her ribs, his thumbs beneath her breasts, his fingers caressing the silky skin of her back. His legs spread, he pulled her into him, close enough that she could see the faint lines radiating from the corner of his silvery eyes.

Her heart stopped, began pounding heavily in her chest as the lassitude of earlier spread throughout her body. She drew in a ragged breath, her hands coming to rest on his strong brown arms.

'Take your top off, you don't need it here.' His voice was husky, low, sexy.

She stared down into his eyes, excitement and desire rising.

Slowly, never taking her eyes from him, she found the first ribbon, fumbled a second and drew it from the bow. The cover-up moved slightly in the breeze. Molly moved to the second ribbon, remembering how Tell had untied them earlier, mimicking his motions, letting the satiny ribbon slide slowly through her fingers. When she reached the third ribbon, Tell gave a low groan.

'You are driving me mad, woman. Will you take it off?'

She smiled, and slowly undid that bow. When the cover-up opened in front, Molly moved to remove it from her shoulders. She held it away from her body, letting it dangle momentarily from her outstretched fingers, then dropping it on the sand.

Tell drew her closer, his mouth moving to kiss her stomach, his tongue flicking briefly against her navel.

Molly moaned softly, her hands coming round to capture his head, holding him briefly against her.

Leaning back, Tell brought her down on top of him, gazing into her eyes with smouldering passion.

'What happened to Miss Prim and Proper?' he asked.

'I think she got lost on the beach . . .' Molly said, moving suggestively against him.

Laughter filtered to them. Looking up in startled awareness, Molly saw a group of five or six people round the headland and start towards the surf. Struggling, she moved to get up, to have Tell release her.

'Damn,' he said, sitting up and glaring at the new-comers. They were too far away to see his expression and gaily waved.

He moved to lie on the hammock and reached for Molly, pulling her down beside him.

'Relax, the fun's over for now. We'll wait until they leave.'

Molly had no choice but to relax against Tell; to remain apart would endanger their precarious balance on the hammock. She was against him from shoulder to thigh, conscious of his body as she had never been before. She closed her eyes, determined to regain her composure, determined to regain control of her emotions and senses before she did something utterly foolish.

Before she realised it, Molly dozed off.

The sun was low on the horizon when Molly awoke. She was sprawled across Tell, her head resting on his chest, one arm thrown over him. Blinking, she sat up to stare down at his familiar mocking smile.

'You're supposed to fall asleep after sex, not before it,' he murmured.

Realisation flooded through her and she scrambled off the hammock, tipping it over and dumping Tell on the sand. Snatching her cover-up, she started towards the pool area at a fast walk, pulling on the white top, tying it firmly with shaking fingers. Maybe she should knot the ties.

'Molly!'

She was not a girl to go in for casual holiday affairs, nor was she so unconcerned with her future that she would tie her life to an indigent cowboy without two cents to his name. Even if he asked her to, which he never had.

'Dammit!' His roar sounded behind her.

Molly quickened her pace.

She reached her things without Tell catching up with her. She was surprised, but didn't stop to wonder what he was doing. She didn't care. She just wanted to get away heart-whole and fancy free. She had no business mixing with that dangerous Texas cowboy.

When she reached the jeep, there was still no sign of him. For a moment she was surprised. With his longer legs he should have overtaken her ages ago. No matter, he'd wanted to come, he came. Now let him find his own way back.

She slammed the jeep in gear and took off, driving just as all the other jeep drivers had, wild, reckless and fast.

Molly half expected Tell to come to the patio that night and she carefully kept to her room, with the air-conditioner on and the curtains closed. Though she peeked out from time to time, she didn't see him.

She refused to be disappointed, though the ache in her breast was very close. She was in Mexico to work, not to spend time with some poor, fun-loving cowboy.

Beverley was still not in the mood to write the next morning, so Molly decided to venture forth into Acapulco. She knew she could find the same car park Beverley had used, and could walk around the city from that point. Since the Avenida Costera Miguel Alemán hugged the beach from one end to the other, she had only to head for the water to find her way back.

Wearing a pair of short navy shorts and a half-top of pink cotton, she considered herself carefully. While not underdressed by Acapulco standards, she was not used to such brevity at home. Still, the sultry heat of the city streets would be better faced like this. Tying her hair up out of the way, she gave a thought to having it cut. It would be more convenient in the climate, and Beverley had intimated that they would stay several weeks. When she thought of Tell's comment, she turned impatiently away from the mirror. She would not cut her hair to suit him!

Molly found the car park with no trouble. She walked down the main street, window-shopping, gazing at the fabulous displays that lined the busy thoroughfare. At one of the large hotels, she paused, made up her mind and went inside.

An hour later she was again walking down the street, her hair in short curls, her head lighter, her neck cooler. She paused before a small mirror, smiling at the sight before her. Was that her? She took off her sunglasses to see better. The curls blew in the afternoon breeze, the tan she'd acquired since arriving gave becoming colour to her face, her blue eyes seemed deeper than ever. She looked almost pretty. Involuntarily, she smiled.

She walked further, smiling at her pleasure in her new look. A man walking towards her smiled broadly in return, winked at her and paused a moment as she walked by, staring unabashedly at her. Molly's spirits rose. Maybe she did look better.

She found her way to the Zócalo, the heart of Acapulco. There were rows and rows of stalls, selling everything from brightly coloured cloth to straw hats, brassware, carved wooden figures. A nearby park offered shade and benches to rest on. But it was the square that was crowded as tourists vied with each other, trying to find the best buys they could. The bustling activity intrigued Molly and she paused, stepping to the side, to watch the action.

When she grew tired of watching, she looked back towards the main street. Her eyes widened. Across the road, just coming from one of the open stalls, was Tell. He was limping. Her puzzled look dropped to his feet; one was wrapped in a snowy white bandage.

'Tell!' she called, moving towards him.

He looked around at the sound of her voice, but didn't recognise her until she was close. His eyes widened when he saw her, his mouth splitting into a big grin. Briefly his gaze flicked down the length of her and Molly was instantly aware that the clothes she wore had been chosen by this man.

'Well, aren't you the pretty girl?' he said, studying the effect of the shorter hair.

She blushed with happiness that he thought so, flushing when recalling his reasons she should get her hair cut.

'I didn't get it cut because you said so,' she said quickly.

'Of course not.' His amusement told her he didn't believe her.

He limped over to stand close to her, his eyes dancing in the sunlight. Audaciously he leaned over and placed a warm kiss on her neck.

'Tell, what happened to your foot?' Her hand reached out and touched his arm, unable to keep away. His skin was warm, the muscles taut.

'I should spank you, Molly. When you ran off so abruptly, I tried to follow you. I cut my foot on some jagged shells. Required two stitches. I'm supposed to be on vacation, not visiting the hospital.'

'Oh, Tell, I'm sorry.'

'So you should be. Why did you leave?' His eyes bore down into hers.

'I ... things ... it was getting ...' She floundered. How to tell him just why she left? She wasn't sure herself.

'Hell, Molly, I told you there'd be no sex if you didn't want it. I've never forced myself on a woman yet and I wouldn't start with you.'

'I didn't think you would,' she said miserably. But at the time she hadn't been so sure. Or had it been her own ability to say no that she doubted?

'If it's the money——' He reached into his pocket.

'No. No, it's not the money. Honestly, Tell, I just had to leave. I'm sorry you got hurt.'

'Getting the sand cleaned out wasn't a picnic, and I can't go in the salt water for a few days, but otherwise it isn't a big deal. What are you doing in town. Is your boss near by?' He looked around the busy marketplace, teeming with all nationalities.

Beverley was so short that she'd be swallowed up in a crowd like this one.

'No. She's visiting friends today. I have the day off.'

Tell's face closed up and he seemed to withdraw. Molly was hurt. Yesterday when she'd told him that she had the day free he'd wanted to spend it with her. Today, he didn't seem to want to be with her. Not that she could blame him—she had been the cause of his injury. She glanced at his foot, wishing she had not been so impetuous yesterday. But she was always wishing that around Tell.

'Shopping, I see,' was all he said.

'I wanted to go sightseeing a little, too. I don't know when I'll have another day off, and thought I'd see some of the sights today.' She stared at him, willing him to ask her to spend the day with him. Longing for his company.

'It's a nice day for it, though it will get hotter later. Enjoy.'

He turned and began to walk down the main street.

Molly watched him go in dismay. She thought he would want to spend time with her. Had he other things planned for today?

'Tell.' She hurried after him. '*Tell*.'

He paused and waited for her to catch up, his eyes drifting over her brief outfit. Molly felt suddenly conscious of how much skin showed.

'Would you like to go with me?' she asked hopefully, breathlessly.

'And have you examined my bank account to make sure I'm acceptable?' he asked, his eyes narrowed, flinty in colour. Molly always knew how he felt by the colour of his eyes—he was angry again.

She flushed with shame, knowing he was referring to her accusation that he was a gigolo. But he'd called *her* a gold-digger...

'My treat,' she said softly. 'Please.'

'No, not your treat. If I go with you, it will be Dutch all the way. I'll pay my own way, you pay yours, exhibits, purchases or food. Agreed?'

She nodded eagerly at his terms. She would agree to almost anything to spend a few more hours in his company. Why was she so mesmerised by this man?

'First thing, then, the *calandrias*.' He placed his hand on the small of her back, guiding her across the pavement and towards one of the gaily decorated horse-drawn carriages lined up at the kerb.

Molly smiled in secret amusement. He'd taken over in less than two seconds. What if she had other plans? She was glad he was with her, however, and would gladly go wherever he suggested. He would know the best places, the sights not to miss. She'd let him take charge. Not that she had much choice in it.

She was enchanted with the carriage, which was shiny and polished, decorated with ribbons and bright balloons. Its horse pawed on the ground as if letting her know he was as anxious as she was to start. Tell handed her up into the open carriage and spoke rapidly in Spanish to the driver. Climbing in after Molly, he sat back beside her.

'A tour of the city. Best way to see it first,' he murmured, looking out as the horse began his walk.

Tell seemed more interested in the sights of Acapulco than in her, but Molly was soon caught up in the tour. She eagerly looked where directed by the driver or Tell, captivated by the contrasting places of the old Mexican city: the glittering high-rise resort hotels, and the old section of town. The shops and market stalls and open-air restaurants vying with the street hawkers selling everything from silver to pretzels. Old-fashioned carriages and modern cars of all types.

Tell took her to La Quebrada, where the cliff divers plunged over one hundred and forty feet into the sea in a narrow, rocky gorge, timing their dives with the surging water. A miscalculation and the diver would be dead. Sipping an iced juice on the veranda of La Mirador, Molly watched with fascinated eyes as the young man accomplished his daring feat. A few minutes later he was walking among the observers, seeking tips. Beaming when he approached her, she gave him a bill. Darting a quick glance at Tell, she saw him give a like amount.

'Dutch all the way,' he murmured, catching her eye as he cocked an eyebrow her way. His gaze held hers for a long moment.

Molly looked away, not sure how to view this. There was none of the overtures he'd given yesterday. They could be total strangers for all the attention he paid to her. Molly was piqued. Yesterday he'd been pushing her, kissing her, urging her to make love to him. Why was he so stand-offish today? She flushed when she realised where her thoughts were going. The reason she'd left so abruptly yesterday was that she'd been scared. Had a day made a difference? Did she want him to kiss her?

The *calandria* took them to the Plaza Juan Alvarez, at the other end of the Zócalo, to see the Acapulco cathedral. It was unusual to Molly with Byzantine towers and a mosque-like dome. Beautiful and ornate, it dominated the Plaza.

El Fuerte De San Diego was the most historic place in Acapulco, a fort built to defend the town when it was a sea port connecting Mexico with the Orient. Molly began to grow tired, but was afraid to let Tell know. She glanced at the usually clear blue sky. It was clouding over. Were they due for some rain? She'd heard of the quick showers that soaked the area for a few hours and then stopped. The sky *was* darkening.

Afraid he'd leave when the tour was over, Molly tried to think of something she could say or do that would let him know she didn't want the day to end when they finished the tour. She didn't know why he was so aloof today. If she had a clue, perhaps she could recapture the earlier friendliness. He hadn't even laughed at her today.

They were almost back at the starting-point, and she still hadn't come up with anything to say that would keep him with her once they finished.

'I've enjoyed seeing the city,' she said, biting her lip when she heard how prim she sounded. But it had done some good; he looked at her with some of the amusement he normally held in his eye.

'I know,' she said, before he could speak. 'Prim and proper again. But I mean it. It was better than going by myself.'

'Glad you enjoyed it.' Now *he* sounded prim and proper. Not at all like the brash Texan she was used to fighting off.

'Is your foot hurting?' she asked.

'Yes, I guess walking around on it wasn't the best thing I could have done. I think I'll call it quits for today and head for camp.'

'Want a ride? I have the jeep.'

He climbed down from the carriage and spoke at length with the driver, giving him a large handful of bills. Molly jumped down and went to stand by him, opening her purse.

'How much is my share?' For a moment she thought he wasn't going to answer her.

'About twelve American dollars.'

She did sums in her head and fished out the foreign currency, carefully counting it out in his hand. Snapping her purse closed, she looked up. '*Do* you want a ride to camp? I could help you with dinner.' There, if he didn't want her around he could say so. She held her breath, afraid he'd do that very thing.

His eyes crinkled in amusement, and he smiled for the first time that afternoon. 'Sure, and that I'd like to see. Where's your jeep?'

Happiness bubbled up inside as Molly led the way to the car park. Her time with Tell wasn't over just yet. She would see where he was staying, and share the evening meal with him. She refused to think beyond that, afraid of where her thoughts would lead her. For now it was enough that she was with Tell Hardin.

CHAPTER SIX

As THEY walked to the car park, Molly noticed that the afternoon breeze was stronger than usual, and cooler. She darted a quick glance at the darkening sky. It looked as if it might rain. She said nothing to Tell, afraid he'd change his mind about letting her come to his camp if he thought it was threatening to rain. And she was exceedingly curious about where he was staying. If he didn't notice himself, she'd not be the one to tell him.

A wolf-whistle broke into Molly's concentration and she looked up, startled to see a young Mexican grinning at her. She smiled shyly back, flattered he'd thought she looked nice. She'd never had someone whistle at her before.

Tell's hand came out to grasp hers and she looked at him in surprise.

'Cutting your hair was a big mistake, I can see that,' he said, glaring at the young man. 'Everyone in Acapulco will be after you now.'

Molly was aglow from his compliment, her heart swelling with delight. She didn't believe him, but was elated that Tell had said it.

'I doubt that,' she murmured, tightening her fingers around his hand, feeling the tough skin of his palm and fingers against the softness of her own. Her arm tingled with his touch and she was suddenly assailed with doubt. Why had she practically invited herself to his camp? What did she think she'd find there?

83

He'd wanted her to come there yesterday, where he'd wanted to make long, slow, passionate love to her. What was he expecting now? She threw him a glance. Did he think she'd changed her mind, now that she agreed to go with him? She bit her lip. Maybe she shouldn't go.

Before she could think of a reasonable excuse, they were in her car and heading out of town. As she followed Tell's directions to his camp, she wondered how he got around the way he did. He was miles from town. They followed one of the mountain roads leading up from the beach area, climbing higher and higher until they were far from the populated area of Acapulco, the area spread behind them like a relief map.

Stopping at a large wooden gate, Tell hopped down from the jeep and swung the gate open. When Molly passed through, he closed it and climbed back into the jeep.

'How do you get to town or to Las Casitas D'Oro?' she asked, turning on to the dirt-road where he directed.

'I have a car I rented.'

'Where is it now?'

'In town.'

She was silent. He had his own transport; he hadn't needed hers. She smiled quietly. He did want to spend some more time with her.

'So after dinner, when you have to go home, you'll have to give me a ride back into town to fetch it,' he murmured, his eyes on her.

She nodded, suddenly afraid to face him. She became conscious of how near he was to her, how alone they were in the pretty little valley that opened up before them. To the east the taller mountains of the Sierra Madre rose, and yet the ridge to the west blotted out all views of Acapulco. They were in their own little world.

She saw the small tent, in a grassy meadow. He motioned her to park near by and they climbed down.

Molly noticed Tell's limp again as he led the way to his camp, and guilt struck her. She hadn't needed to panic yesterday, and run off the way she'd done—he hadn't threatened her; it was herself she was afraid of. Yet it was her fault he'd cut his foot. She'd try to make it up to him. She could cook dinner, at least.

But Tell would let her do nothing. He sat her near the fire and talked to her as he worked quickly and efficiently. She watched, fascinated, as he built the fire, started a stew for dinner and even baked a small apple crumb cake for dessert. He made it look so easy. She knew she could never have managed so well.

The food was delicious and Tell kept her entertained with stories of his childhood in south Texas along the Rio Grande.

'So there were five of you,' Molly said at one point, trying to keep all the brothers and sisters straight.

'In my immediate family, but I have dozens of cousins. And aunts and uncles and grandparents—everyone is always dropping by, so it's hard to tell who lives there and who doesn't.'

'What do your brothers and sisters do now?' she asked as she finished the last of her cake. She wished there were more. But the coffee was delicious and she settled back to sip that while Tell told her more.

'One brother's a ... cowboy, like me. The other is in the Air Force. One sister is a lawyer, the other a homemaker, with three kids already. I don't think they're stopping at that, either.'

'Are they all married?'

'No, just the Captain, and Diane.'

'And where are you?'

'Here.'

'No,' she giggled softly, smiling up into his eyes. 'I mean, where in birth order, oldest?'

'Yep. How about you?'

Molly's smile faded. She didn't have fun stories to tell of her childhood, nor of any part of her life. She had to work too hard to keep going. 'I'm an only. An orphan, as a matter of fact. My folks died when I was young.' She sipped her coffee, her eyes on the fire.

'And?' he prompted.

'I was sent to live with distant relatives, but that didn't work out, so then it was foster homes.'

'That's tough.' His voice was soft, sympathetic. She refused to look at him, or feel sorry for herself.

'If you do things right, you get to stay?' he hazarded a guess, and Molly looked up, startled. How had he known?

She nodded slowly.

'I can't imagine anyone not wanting you to stay with them,' he said, holding her eyes with his own. 'If you had to move, it wasn't because you were bad or did something wrong—probably economics.'

'Maybe. Anyway, that's why security is so important to me. I need to know I won't end up like my mother, destitute and with a kid to support.'

Without warning a gust of wind blew across the field, a torrent of cold rain immediately following. Molly had not given a thought to the threat of rain since she'd arrived. The sky was dark, and looked as if the storm had been building for some time, but she and Tell had been caught up in their conversation, not paying attention to the weather.

Gasping in the shock of the deluge, Molly scrambled up, looking wildly for shelter. They were some yards from the tent, further from the jeep, and it had no top. Tell grabbed her hand and hurried over to the small tent, running as fast as his injured foot would allow. Molly couldn't see three yards in front of her; the rain was pouring down, cold and wet, the wind blowing it every which way.

In only seconds she was soaked to the skin, her hair dripping in her face, her legs streaked with water and splattered with mud.

They huddled just inside the opening, looking over at the fire, which was being extinguished by the water falling from the heavens. The twilight was fading fast, hastened no doubt by the storm.

Molly shivered; she was soaked!

'Boy, that was quick. I noticed earlier that it looked as if it might storm, but forgot about it while talking to you. I have some towels—wait while I find them. And get a light.'

Tell moved away.

Molly couldn't see him in the dark, couldn't see anything in the tent, the light from outside too faint. But she could hear him moving through his things. A strong torch suddenly illuminated their shelter and she saw Tell offer her a fluffy yellow towel.

Molly dried her dripping hair and mopped up the water from her arms and legs. Her skimpy top clung to her like a second skin, clammy and cold. Her shorts were wet, too. She shivered slightly in the damp air, the temperature already dropping.

'How long do you think it'll last?' she asked, wiping the rain from her glasses, laying them near the opening, out of the way. Should she try to drive home now? She couldn't get any wetter.

'Don't know—an hour or two. It'll blow over before midnight.'

'I'm cold.'

'Me, too. Wet clothes do that. The temperature will drop even more with the rain. We can change into dry things—it'll help. If you're still cold after that, well, I know something to warm you up.'

Molly stared at him in the faint illumination, heat rising in her cheeks. She knew to what he was alluding, but refused to rise to the bait.

'I don't have any other clothes.'

'I have some you can wear.' Tell threw her a blue denim work shirt, long-sleeved. 'Try that.'

Molly knelt in the dirt and stared at him. The tent wasn't more than seven feet long nor more than four or five feet wide. Just where was she to change into this shirt?

Tell drew off his shirt and tossed it into a sodden heap near the opening, pulling on a sweatshirt. When he raised his hips and unzipped his cut-offs, Molly turned and looked out on the rainy landscape, biting her lip, shivering a little. She was cold.

'Quite a dilemma for Miss Prim and Proper, isn't it?' The mocking tone was back in his voice. Molly thought she hated him at that moment.

Resolutely, she shook out his shirt and laid it across her knees. With her back to him, she drew her pink top over her head and tossed it to join his shirt. She unfastened her wet bra, and it followed suit. She quickly drew on his shirt and buttoned it up in front,

to the top. She raised herself on her knees and unfastened her shorts. Her panties were of nylon and
would dry in minutes. These she left on, easing the
shorts down and off. Refusing to turn around to face
Tell, she slowly rolled up the huge sleeves so that her
hands could be free. What was she going to do? How
long would the rain last? Would he try to make love
to her? Her blood surged through her veins at the
thought. He didn't need to for her to warm up; the
mere thought of it accomplished that!

'Are you still cold?' his soft voice asked in her left
ear, as his hands took hold of her shoulders and his
lips left fiery kisses on her neck.

She nodded, afraid to speak. Gently, he pulled her
back against him, until she was resting against his
warm chest, his knees on either side of her legs. His
arms came around and crossed over her, just beneath
her breasts, as he enveloped her in his warmth. Resting
his chin on her shoulder, he held her and they looked
out through the opening at the rain on the field.

Molly remained still, savouring the feel of his body
against hers, his arms enclosing her. It was heavenly.

'How will I get home?' she asked.

'The rain won't last for long. When it's blown over,
we'll dry off the seats in the jeep and be set. I still
need to get my car.'

She stirred and pulled away, afraid to remain in such
proximity any longer. Her thoughts were no longer
about going home, and that was dangerous.

'So what do we do until then?' The rain was coming
down as strongly as ever. Would it really end within
a few hours?

'You can tell me more about you and I can tell you more about me. But we can be more comfortable if we sit on the sleeping-bag. This dirt is hard.'

Tell moved away and Molly could hear him pulling things in the background. Reluctantly, she turned from the opening and watched him. He spread open his sleeping-bag, tossed his duffel bag to one side. The soft glow of the powerful torch gave warmth to the tent.

Tell sprawled out on the sleeping-bag, lying on one elbow, and watched Molly. His lips turned up slightly as he took in her appearance. The denim shirt fitted her like a short dress that was much too big for her. Her hair was still damp but beginning to curl, and she was kneeling, sitting back on her heels.

'The shirt looks better on you than me,' he said, his eyes a silvery grey. 'But you look like a nun with it buttoned to the top. Unfasten it.' His voice was low, sexy, seductive. Molly stared at him, fascinated by the look in his eyes, the smoky, smouldering stare he gave her as he waited for her to obey his command. She licked her lips, her heart beginning to beat rapidly. With nerveless fingers, she raised her hand and slowly slipped the first button through the hole. She couldn't look away.

Tell's eyes never left hers as they narrowed in assessment. 'Do another.'

Was she hypnotised that she couldn't look away, couldn't function on her own? Slowly she slid the second button through the material. The heat pulsating through her body warmed her, making her intensely aware of the man lying carelessly across his sleeping-bag only a few feet away. Her eyes couldn't leave his; they were compelling, irresistible, seductive.

'Another.'

She took a shaky breath and slid another through the material, wondering if he would have her open the entire front of the shirt.

Molly was conscious of the cotton material touching her, enfolding her, caressing her. It had last touched Tell's shoulders and chest; now it warmed her own skin. She felt a peculiar delight spread throughout her body. Dared she moved to join him on the sleeping-bag? The ground was hard against her legs, but she was afraid to move.

The material separated slightly, the skin exposed hinting at curves in the shadows.

With almost a groan, Tell sat up and reached out for her, drawing her to him on the sleeping-bag. He wrapped his arms around her and crushed her against his chest. Molly resisted for only a moment, then lay compliant against him. She loved the strength of the man, the excitement and daring she felt around him.

Tell lay back, pulling part of the sleeping-bag over Molly to keep the chilled air from her bare legs.

'OK?' he asked, stroking her damp hair.

She could scarcely breathe, much less talk. Every inch of her skin was attuned to Tell, longing for him to touch her, longing for the feel of his skin against hers, his mouth against hers.

'No.' She struggled away from him, pulling back and scooting across the opened sleeping-bag. Eyes wide, she stared back at a startled Tell. How could she tell him she just couldn't allow herself to become taken with a drifting cowboy? She'd had a hard life and she didn't want to make any mistakes that would perpetuate that. If she became involved with a man, it would be with someone who was established, who could provide her with the basics of security.

'Now what?' His tone was exasperated.

'I . . . nothing. I . . . if we are going to talk, we can talk. I'm warm now,' she lied, holding herself still against the chill that engulfed her.

Tell was silent, watching her through narrow, assessing eyes, no longer silvery, but a hard steel-grey. Molly forced herself to meet his gaze, though she was trembling inside. After a moment, he shrugged and flicked off the torch.

'Save the battery,' he murmured.

The rain steadily assaulted the tent, its noise a soothing steady pattern. The air was growing cooler and the last vestiges of daylight faded.

Molly settled in the spot she was in and tried to see Tell in the darkness. She could barely make out his shape.

'So tell me more, Molly, about being shunted around as a child,' Tell invited.

'There's not much to tell. I didn't have the fun you did.' Molly remembered the frightened feeling she'd had when her mother had died. Who would take care of her, who would ever love her again? She had only been eight, and left all alone. Her mother had often worried aloud about their fate, money had been so scarce and hard to come by. She'd often told Molly she didn't know where their next meal would come from.

Molly knew now that her mother should not have burdened a young child with her fears, but at the time Molly had only been afraid.

'So who raised you?' Tell asked.

'I went to live with cousins at first. I was eight. They weren't very kind. They didn't like being burdened with me. So a year or so later they turned me over to the state and I lived in a series of foster homes until I was eighteen.'

Her voice was calm, matter-of-fact. Not for anything would she let Tell know of the hurt and despair she'd felt all those years. The fear of not having a place to stay, food to eat. Of never knowing the love and care she'd felt from her mother. She had made it on her own, but she knew that, should she wish to marry, she would have to do so with a man who could provide for her and any children they might have, not someone like her father, a charming man, unskilled at anything but having a good time. Or so her mother had always said. When he had died, he had left nothing but debts. They had been married so young; neither had education or training beyond a high-school diploma. Molly wouldn't repeat her parents' mistake. Not for her a charming, drifting cowboy, who didn't even have enough money to stay in a cheap motel.

'A series?'

'Yes, almost one each school year. I did stay with one family for two years. But then they moved and I couldn't go with them. My childhood isn't as fun to think back on as yours, Tell.'

The rain was slowing. Molly cocked her head. Maybe it'd stop soon. Let her get back to the hotel, back to her quiet life, end this craziness with Tell. She should not have come.

'That explains your desire to marry a rich man,' Tell said softly.

'I don't want to marry a rich man,' she said sharply, 'but if I marry I want it to be a man who has a steady income, a skill that can be counted on. I don't want to be left destitute if he dies, or leave any children in the circumstances I was.'

'So again, show your bank balance to the lady before she will become involved.' His voice had a hard edge.

'No, I don't need to see anyone's bank book, but I want to know there's security. This is the same argument we had the other night.'

'Yes, and I don't think we've gotten anywhere. Do you want to see my bank book?'

'Do you have one?' Sarcasm dripped from her tone.

'Not on me, but I can get it sent here,' he bit out.

'Don't bother. I'm sure you're nicely situated, for a cowboy. What do you do when you get old? I've never seen old cowboys. Do they have retirement homes for them?'

Tell sat up and moved towards her.

'You may not live to see anyone old with a sharp tongue like yours. I'll make out just fine, Miss Prim and Proper Gold-digger. The rain has stopped—come on, let's go.'

He reached for her in the dark and drew her towards the flap. Thrusting it open, Molly grabbed her glasses, and they were standing on the damp grass of the meadow. The air was crystal-clear and clean. It was like drinking wine to breathe it. The wind had died. The night was still black as pitch, the last of the clouds obscuring the stars.

Tell switched on the torch and ran it over her. She blinked in the sudden light, and turned slightly. As the light travelled the length of her, she looked down.

The shirt covered her to mid-thigh, the sleeves hung down below her wrists, even rolled up. It covered more of her than her lacy white cover-up, but she felt vulnerable in it. It was Tell's. There was a certain intimacy implied in wearing his clothes.

'Come on.' His voice was impersonal, impatient.

Tell strode off ahead and Molly hurried to keep up, not wanting to get too far behind and lose the light.

He used a towel to wipe off the seats and climbed into the driver's seat.

'I'll drive; toss me the keys.'

They returned to Acapulco in silence. Tell spoke only when asking her to open and close the wooden gate. Molly complied, afraid even to suggest he do it himself. He seemed to be in a black mood, but she wouldn't chance finding out why. She thought she knew.

He drew up beside a black Ford Fiesta.

'This is my car. I'll follow you back to Las Casitas D'Oro to make sure you get back safely.'

She nodded, wanting to apologise, wanting things to be different. But she'd already said things she couldn't recall and nothing would really change even if she could.

She drove carefully back to the hotel, conscious of the twin lights behind her, of Tell watching out for her. She felt safe, cherished almost. She wished things had been different, wished he had money and a steady job so she could let herself fall in love...

What was she thinking of? She couldn't wish for the moon and have everything come her way. It never had. She was no longer a little girl, wishing for a fairy-tale life. She was grown and realistic. Tell was not for her. He'd never given any indication of wanting anything more than a light dalliance while on holiday. She had better remember that and let herself be guided appropriately.

When Molly reached her room, she could hear Beverley talking in the adjacent room, dictating again. Tomorrow would be work as normal. And Molly was glad. It would give her something to do, take her mind off Tell Hardin.

CHAPTER SEVEN

DESPITE Molly's belief in reality, she slept in Tell's shirt, imagining he was wrapped around her as the soft blue denim was. When she awoke the next morning, she felt lonely and sad. She wished she could let go of her need for security, grab what happiness life might offer and look forward to the future without worry or fear.

But she couldn't. She had to plan and make sure she would be better prepared for whatever came her way than her mother had been.

She walked out on to the patio promptly at eight. Beverley was already sitting beside the pool, sipping a cup of the rich coffee the hotel provided. She smiled brightly at Molly.

'All rested and ready for work?'

Molly smiled back, glad that routine would take over. She'd had too much time off. Work was safer. She sank on a chair near the table and reached for a cup.

'Sure am. Did I hear you dictating last night?'

'Yes, I was on a roll and didn't finish until late. I have about three tapes for you to get started on and can do several more today. I know just what I'm going to reveal about our friend today and can't wait to get started. Pershing was such an interesting man—I don't think everyone knows that and I hope I can help some people discover that fact.' She nodded in time with her speaking and Molly was again reminded of a little bird.

'Tonight, though, we're taking a break. I know it's dull for you here, with no friends and all. The Alverado family has invited us to dinner. They're old friends of mine. You'll like them. They have a son and daughter just about your age, so you'll meet some young people here. Maybe have a chance to go somewhere.'

It was on the tip of Molly's tongue to tell Beverley about her meeting Tell, but she held back. Beverley had been very specific that she didn't think Molly should have anything to do with Tell Hardin. And Molly didn't want to take the chance of upsetting her boss by telling her she hadn't listened to her advice.

Besides, after last night, would Tell want to see her again?

'I don't really have anything to wear to a dinner party,' Molly said softly, thinking of the practical clothes she'd brought, and the new casual ones she'd bought.

'Well, we'll take a break this afternoon and you can dash down to the little shop near the lobby. They have some nice dresses.'

Which would cost the earth, Molly thought. Her funds were meagre now, and she wasn't to be paid for another few days. Well, she'd look, anyway. If she couldn't find anything, she would just tell Beverley she couldn't go.

When she'd finished eating, Molly went to get the tapes Beverley had already done. Sitting before the computer, she was soon caught up in the life and times of General Black Jack Pershing.

Several times during the morning, Molly's mind would wander from the tapes and end up thinking about Tell. She'd see his face before her, his dancing grey eyes, his mocking smile. Then she'd remember the kisses he'd given her at the beach and she'd grow warm, distracted. He filled her thoughts; it was hard to marshal them in other directions.

Shaking her head to clear it, she'd attack the work furiously, trying to forget. But sooner or later her mind would remember.

'Are you all right?' Beverley asked at one point, looking at her strangely.

Molly looked up, flushed. She nodded, wary of giving anything away.

'You looked distracted.' Beverley watched her secretary from her dark eyes. 'Not getting sick, Montezuma's revenge?'

'No, I'm fine.' Molly tried to concentrate on the words in her ears, transcribing them to the computer. She *would not* think of Tell again!

After a light lunch of salad, crackers and iced tea, Molly again returned to work. She would take a break when the stores opened after siesta and see if the shop near the lobby had anything she could afford. She set herself a goal of two more tapes finished by then. Forcing herself to concentrate, she didn't think of Tell all afternoon, until she started walking towards the shop.

Wondering what kind of dress she might be able to afford, she fantasised about buying a beautiful dress that would drive Tell wild with desire and passion. It would be nice to have him see her all dressed up, instead of in the resort attire or the business suit from Los Angeles.

But her dream faded as she looked at the dresses on the racks. It was as she feared; they were expensive, some of them hundreds of dollars. There were few in her size, and all too expensive for her purse. It was fun to look at them, imagine Tell seeing her in them. What would his reaction be?

'Can I help you, *señorita*?' The assistant was elegantly dressed, unlike those in the shops along the Avenida Costera Miguel Alemán. Much better dressed than Molly could afford to be.

'I was looking for a dress to wear to a dinner party, but everything here is more than I care to spend,' she said, moving dresses on the rod.

'Our selection in your size is quite limited, unfortunately. There is an excellent shop in the Continental Hotel; perhaps they'd have something for you.'

Molly smiled. 'My time is limited. I'm working and was hoping to dash in and find something.'

She looked past the assistant, and saw the dress for her. It was a blue like the sky over Acapulco, with a halter neck, fitted bodice and a flaring skirt. It was hanging over a rack by the register.

'How about that one? Is it in my size?' Molly knew it would be too expensive, yet it was perfect.

'Oh, *qué lástima*, it is ripped. We are not selling it. It is a beautiful gown, *sí*?' The woman brought it over to Molly, who touched the silky material, loving the feel of it. She could see the tear, on the skirt, on the side.

'It could be mended,' she said softly, reaching for it to hold it in front of her. She moved before the mirror. Her eyes sparkled, their colour enhanced by the soft blue of the dress. Her cheeks were rosy, her lips glossy. She wished Tell could see her in this dress.

'We do not sell goods that need to be mended.' The assistant was kind.

'I'd buy it and fix it. It would be a wonderful dress to have. Please.'

The woman hesitated.

'It's good business to make some money, even if it is not as much as you would have made had the dress not been ripped,' Molly pressed.

'You are correct, *señorita*, some money is better than a loss. *Sí*, I will sell it to you.'

Molly almost hugged herself with glee as she walked back up the hill to the *casita*. The dress had been cut to one-third the original price. It had still cost more than Molly usually spent on a dress, but had been affordable. A few minutes with a needle and thread and it would be perfect.

Molly flew through the work remaining, anticipation building for the evening ahead. She'd meet Beverley's friends, enjoy herself. It would be nice to get out and see some of the real Mexico, instead of the tourist spots.

She longed to see Tell, but told herself it would be pointless. He'd just laugh at her anyway, all dressed up. But she wished that he could see her in the pretty dress, just once.

It fitted as though it had been made with her in mind. The high halter neck bared her arms and shoulders, her creamy tanned skin a perfect foil. It was low in the back, but hugged her waist like a second skin. The skirt flared around her legs, skimming the tops of her knees.

Putting on her make-up carefully, Molly decided to leave her glasses at home. She could see close up and wouldn't be so self-conscious if she couldn't see all the people at the party. Besides, glasses ruined the effect of the dress.

When she and Beverley arrived at the Alverado villa, Molly was struck by its size. Easily twice the size of an average house in the States, it was situated on a bluff overlooking Acapulco Bay. The front windows framed the view as though a fine artist had positioned it. The lights were coming on across the water and the picture was breathtaking. She wished for a moment she'd worn her glasses to see the view properly.

There were already about a dozen people gathered on the front patio, a liveried waiter circulated with glasses of champagne. More people were coming behind them. Molly had thought it a quiet dinner among friends, not a party. She spoke no Spanish— would she be able to communicate at all?

'Beverley, it is so good to see you.' A tall, distinguished gentleman approached them. Beverley smiled up and greeted him as their host.

'Juan, I'd like to present Molly Spencer. She's my new assistant. Priscilla got married, the naughty girl.'

'Welcome, Señorita Spencer. *Mi casa es tu casa.*' He bowed in a courtly manner.

Molly smiled shyly. 'How do you do? I was afraid for a moment I would be unable to communicate. I'm sorry, but I don't speak Spanish.'

'It is of no matter. Most of the guests here tonight will speak some English. I will assure you that we will have someone with you who can translate, should you wish to converse with anyone who cannot speak English. I'm happy you came.'

He turned and searched the crowd, calling when he found the man he wanted. 'Luis!'

The young man excused himself from the group he was with and moved gracefully towards Juan.

'*Sí*?'

'Luis, I'd like to present Molly Spencer, an associate of our friend Beverley. Señorita Spencer does not speak Spanish. Perhaps you could introduce her around and make sure she is looked after.' The older man smiled at Molly. 'Luis is my son.'

'*Sí*, Papa, my pleasure. How do you do, Señorita Spencer?'

'Very well, thank you.' Molly briefly studied the young man before her. He was slim, tall, and quite immaculately turned out. His eyes were dark brown and friendly. He smiled and offered her his arm.

Taking it, Molly stepped beside him, and soon they were walking around the reception area. Molly was introduced to almost everyone there. When they'd completed the introductions he felt necessary, Luis took her to the far edge of the patio and seated her at one of the tables.

'Duty done, I can now devote the rest of the evening to you. What would you like to drink? A Planter's Punch, perhaps?'

'What's that?'

'Fruit juices with rum—light, refreshing.'

'I'd like to try it, it sounds good.'

He was back in only moments, two tall glasses in his hand. When Molly sipped hers, she smiled.

'It's perfect.'

'*Bueno*; now tell me all about you, Señorita Spencer. You have not been long with Beverley or I would have met you before this.'

'No, just the last several weeks.'

'And the work, how do you like it?'

Molly lost her shyness around Luis and found it easy to talk with him. She liked her job and was easily persuaded to talk about it. And about her liking for Mexico. 'It's beautiful here; is all your country so lovely?'

'I, of course, think so. We have a home in Mexico City as well. There is a different beauty there, but it is lovely. Maybe one day you can come and visit us there.'

Molly smiled, knowing she never would. 'Maybe.'

'Have you seen much of Acapulco?' Luis asked, his eyes studying the pretty girl across from him, never distracted by the other guests circulating.

'I have seen the beaches, and some of the sight-seeing places, the Zócala, the cathedral, La Quebrada.'

Talking about her tour brought Tell to mind. Without meaning to do so, Molly found herself comparing Luis to Tell. The man before her was obviously wealthy, accustomed to fine things. The house was exquisitely decorated, with valuable *objets d'art*, expensive Persian rugs and fine furniture. Luis's clothes were tailored to perfection. He wore a gold ring on his right hand and the Rolex at his wrist was costly.

Yet, charming and attentive as Luis was, Molly missed Tell. She'd rather have him sitting across from her, with his mocking eyes, as she took in all the beauty of Luis's home. He'd put her firmly in her place, scoff at her for being impressed with riches, and be so devastatingly attractive that she'd lose sight of any other man in the room.

'What are you thinking, Molly? Your face is very expressive.' Luis smiled kindly.

She coloured slightly and looked away; Tell had told her the same thing.

Across the room she spotted a tall man dressed in a dark suit. For a second she thought it was Tell. Then a couple of baseball devotees came before her, arguing about a score, and she looked away. What would Tell be doing at the Alverados'? She glanced back at Luis and smiled.

'I was thinking how lovely your view is. Would a person ever grow blasé with this view, ever take it for granted?' She hoped that would cover her. Was it Tell she'd seen?

Luis swung around to look at it and turned back to tell her of how his grandfather had first built the villa, long before Acapulco was world-famous, how his family had always spent winters and fiesta-time in Acapulco.

Molly was content to listen to him talk, learn something of how a Mexican family lived. As the evening progressed, she searched the guests, but didn't see the tall man again.

'I'm about ready to leave—how are you doing?' Beverley hurried over to Molly, smiling brightly at Luis.

'Why don't you take Molly out, Luis? She's getting dull just sitting around with an old lady like me. She needs to get out and meet some people.'

'Oh, no. I'm fine, really,' Molly protested, laughing nervously. 'I've seen lots of the sights. Luis doesn't have to bother...'

'Ah, but it would be no bother; it would give me great pleasure. Perhaps dinner the evening after tomorrow? We can go to one of the discos in town when we are finished. It would be my pleasure.'

'Oh, I don't think…the work and all.' Molly knew it was a lame excuse.

'Nonsense! Of course she can go. Come to Las Casitas D'Oro about eight, Luis. I'll see she's ready. We're near the top, Casita 284. Lovely to see you again. Do you want to wait until later, Molly?'

'No, I'm ready when you are.' Things were going too fast for her. She didn't want to go out with Luis, didn't want him to feel obliged to take her out. But how could she get out of it when they only meant to be kind?

She'd have to go. And she'd rather not. Luis was nice, but he wasn't anyone special. She'd had a pleasant evening tonight, but didn't need to be wined and dined by Luis.

She refused to think what she'd rather be doing. And with whom.

The next two days were idyllic. Molly rose early, and ate breakfast on the patio overlooking the large blue bay. Two cruise ships came in, their horns loud in the morning stillness. She watched them dock and imagined the flurry of activity on board as everyone prepared to visit Acapulco.

Trying to keep up with Beverley was hard. The woman talked constantly, tape recorder in hand, dictating tape after tape. Molly's speed increased, her accuracy increased, and still she fell behind.

When she took a break, she'd swim, lie in the sun and dream about Tell Hardin. She'd not seen nor heard from him since the night of the rainstorm. Would she ever see him again? She knew she made him mad with her desire for security, but still wanted to see him again. She felt listless and bored. Was this how she would feel when they left Acapulco and she never saw him again?

For a moment her heart stopped, then began pounding. She felt sick. She didn't want to think about that. Knowing it would come, still she wanted to postpone the moment as long as she could. Maybe Tell would show up again tonight.

The second day she finished work and took another quick swim before beginning her preparations for the evening's dinner. She was a fool to keep remembering Tell; she'd do better to cultivate someone like Luis. He had charm, looks, manners and money. What more could a woman want in a mate?

By the time dinner was halfway over, Molly had her answer. She wanted excitement.

Luis was nice, kind, polite, charming. But he was not interesting to her. His talk of his work in the city was boring. She didn't care about Mexico City nor the businesses there. She was only visiting this country. She'd be going home soon. She didn't care about the *coups* he'd pulled off, or the large deals he was working on. Money still played an important part of her decision for a life partner, but excitement would also have to be present.

The rest of the evening passed pleasantly enough. They finished dinner and went to Baby-O, one of the frolicking discos that came to life after dark. Dancing eliminated the ability to think and Molly had a fine time. It was late when they reached the hotel.

'Thank you, Luis. I enjoyed myself,' she said politely as she prepared to leave his car.

'It was my pleasure. Unfortunately, I am leaving for Mexico City in the morning—that deal I was telling

you about. It may be some time before I can return
to Acapulco. May I call you when I do?'

'If we're still here. I don't know exactly how long
Beverley plans to stay.'

'I will call anyway.'

He walked her to her door, kissed her lightly on
her cheek and bade her a pleasant goodnight.

Molly smiled as she let herself into her room. The
evening had been enjoyable, but if Luis didn't return
from Mexico City before they left she wouldn't miss
him. He was charming company and made sure she'd
had a good time. But she had no strong desire to spend
any more time with him.

Molly switched on her lights and dropped her bag
on her bed. Walking to the sliding glass doors, she
drew them open. She'd take a quick look over the bay
before retiring. It was a view she never tired of and
wanted to store up memories for the long years ahead.
She would probably never return to Acapulco.

From habit her eyes went to the far corner—and
stopped when she saw Tell in one of the chairs.

'Tell.' She darted a glance to the room next to hers.
It was dark. Had Beverley gone to sleep? The curtain
was drawn—maybe so.

Quickly Molly walked around the pool, over to
where Tell sat watching her.

'Hello, Molly.' He remained seated, looking out
over the bay.

'What are you doing here?' Her heart soared.

'Brought your clothes back. The ones that got wet
in the rain.' He motioned to the neatly folded clothes
on the table near him. 'Thought I'd say hi. Though
I've been here for hours.'

'I was out.' She sat on the edge of the chair nearest him and looked at him in the dim light.

'Dinner and dancing by the looks of it.' He turned to run his eyes over her.

She had worn the blue dress again, and was glad Tell could see her in it, wished he could see her properly. Would he think it suited her?

'Yes, with someone who invited me and paid for the both of us,' she snapped. She didn't want to talk about her evening with Tell.

'Who with?'

'A friend of Beverley's. Luis Alverado.'

'Well, well, well, Miss Prim and Proper did all right for herself.' His taunting voice hit her like a fist.

Molly felt her anger rise. 'What do you mean?'

'Luis Alverado is quite a catch. I bet you never even asked to see his bank balance. He shows off his wealth all the time.'

'I didn't go out with him for that!'

'Of course you did, why else?'

'Beverley wanted me to have a good time and suggested I go out.'

'And have you been having an awful time?'

'No. I...but she doesn't know I've seen you a couple of times.'

'That's right, we don't want to go against her wishes. She might fire you and then where would you be?'

'Where I don't expect to be. I'm working hard at this job and I think I can keep it.'

'Unless Beverley finds out you're seeing me, after she said you shouldn't.'

Molly looked away, suddenly depressed. It was true; how would Beverley react to the fact Molly had been seeing Tell? She still didn't know Beverley well enough to judge her reactions to Molly's ignoring her advice. Would she laugh and pass it off, or become angry?

Tell sighed and rose.

'Where are you going?' Molly stood. She'd longed to see him for two days; surely he could stay a little longer.

'Back to camp. I brought the clothes; that's all I came for.'

'Don't go. How's your foot?' She desperately wanted him to stay a while longer.

'Healing. Why should I stay?' He stepped closer to her, tilted her head up to his gaze.

'No glasses? Luis rated special attention. Did he find you beautiful and ravishing?'

'He said I looked nice.' Molly could scarcely speak above the tightness in her throat as she gazed into the shimmering silver of Tell's eyes. His hand at her chin burned into her skin, her knees grew weak and she longed to reach out to him for support.

'"Nice" is too insipid for you, my proper little friend. How were his kisses, hot like mine? Or gentle and polite?'

'He only kissed me on the cheek,' she whispered, drowning in his gaze, her spirits rising.

'More fool he,' Tell said as he lowered his mouth against hers, holding back as his lips touched hers, as if he waited for a signal from her.

Molly moved against him, encircling his neck with her arms and pressing herself against the length of his hard body.

He held her tightly against him and opened her mouth, his tongue plunging deep within the moisture of her, exploding passion within her so Molly thought she'd die. She duelled with him, meeting thrust with thrust, following his tongue back into his mouth, daringly offering him the pleasure he'd offered her.

She could scarcely breathe, the feeling she was experiencing threatening to overwhelm her. She could only feel Tell, the thickness of his hair, the hot passion of his mouth, the wild beating of his heart against hers.

He bent and picked her up in his arms, moving to sit carefully on the nearby chair. His mouth never left hers and Molly relaxed against him. When one arm came around her, she moved against his chest. His hand found the open back of her dress and paused. He drew back.

'No back?'

Impatiently she shook her head.

'No, it only fastens at the neck,' she said against his lips, not wanting to miss a second of his kisses. She moved easily against him when his hand slipped across her spine to caress the satin skin of her back.

'And no bra?' His breath mingled with hers as he brushed hot kisses across her mouth.

She shook her head, her mouth against his, her hand massaging, caressing the strong muscles of his neck, sliding down to rub across his chest.

Her nails lightly raked themselves across one nipple, and Tell drew in his breath sharply. His other hand pushed up under her skirt, rubbing the silky skin of her thigh, softly, in circles, each time drawing closer and closer to the core of her.

Molly couldn't think, she could only feel and respond to eternal instincts. She grew hot and fevered, longing for more, yearning for Tell to bring her to the heights of ecstasy, the heights of delight and pleasure.

He stood with her in his arms and started across the patio. For a moment Molly thought to stop him, but then changed her mind. For one magical night she'd sleep in his arms. She knew she couldn't build a life with him, but she'd at least have one magical night.

CHAPTER EIGHT

TELL set her on her feet on the terrazzo floor of her room. Molly blinked up at him in the bright room light.

Molly was in a daze; looking over his shoulder at the mirror, she stared at herself for a few seconds. Was that really her? Her skin was flushed and becoming, her eyes bright and sparkling and her hair a soft cloud around her face. She looked pretty. Smiling timorously, she let her eyes drift to meet his.

Tell was standing just inside the door, his tanned chest rising and falling as if he'd been running. Molly felt better; she wasn't the only one affected by their kissing.

The sudden rap on the door startled her. She dropped her arms and spun around. Who could it be at this time of night? She peered at her clock; it looked as if it was after midnight.

Tell stepped up beside her, leaning over to speak softly in her ear.

'Who is it?'

'I don't know.'

The rap came again. 'Molly? Are you in there?'

It was Beverley Sampson.

'Damn!' Tell breathed. He kissed Molly on the cheek. 'You've got to let her in.' He moved back out of the sliding doors.

Molly walked to the front door of her room and opened it slightly, then all the way.

'I was hoping you were back and hadn't just left the light on. I left my purse at one of the places I stopped in tonight and didn't have my key. I didn't want to have to drive all the way back down tonight and when I saw your bathroom light on a minute ago I thought you must be home. Did you and Luis have a good time? You can't have been home long—you're still dressed.'

Beverley bustled into Molly's room and sank on the chair.

'I've only been home for a few minutes,' Molly said, darting a swift glance towards the patio. She saw no sign of Tell. Would Beverley suspect anything? Molly's lips felt swollen from Tell's kisses; could Beverley see that? And if she did, would she think it was from Luis?

'Well, I hope you don't mind me sleeping in with you tonight. I don't know where I left my purse and I hate to have to go down to the lobby. This will make the third key I've lost and they get so tiresome when they have to change the locks. You have a big bed— we can share, can't we?'

Molly's heart dropped, and she sank down on the edge of the large bed Beverley spoke of. Only moments ago, she had thought to share it with Tell; now she would be sharing it with Beverley. She wondered if Tell was in hearing distance. And how he was feeling if he was.

'Sure, it's a big bed. I have an extra nightie that will fit you, too.' Molly smiled. There was no help for it.

When Beverley went into the bathroom to change and prepare for bed, Molly slipped out to the patio.

Tell was leaning against the wall. She walked over to him.

'I guess you heard.'

He smiled down at her and drew a finger along her jaw.

'Yeah, I heard. Damn the old woman for being so forgetful. Want to come back with me to my camp?' he asked, his eyes mocking her. He already knew the answer.

She smiled back at him, knowing he was teasing her.

'No.'

She wanted him to come again, but didn't want to appear forward by asking him. Silently she stood and watched him.

'You'd better get back inside. I'll see you.'

'You'll come again?' she ventured, unable to help herself.

'One of these days. You want to go riding along the beach?'

'I don't know when I'll have a day off again.'

'Just let Miguel know.'

She was disappointed. She'd thought he could come by to find out. But maybe he had other plans. The feeling left her sad, frustrated, unsettled.

'Goodnight, Molly.' He leaned over and kissed her softly. Like the first night, he faded into the darkness. She couldn't hear him leave, but knew he was gone. Slowly she returned to her bedroom and soon to bed.

'Luis is so charming, I always thought,' Beverley said the next morning as they shared croissants and coffee on the patio. The day was bright and warm, the breeze still. It would grow hot before the sun was much higher.

Molly didn't want to think about Luis Alverado; she'd much rather remember Tell's kisses of last night, the feel of his hands on her back and the delight she'd thought they would share. In the bright light of day she was relieved she had not given in to the passion that had built between them. She should curtail her involvement with him totally. He was not for her. He'd never even suggested he was. All along he'd been up front with her. He was on holiday. He obviously had very little money. He was not the man for her.

She wanted a stable, established man. One who could provide security for her and any children they might have. Until and unless she found such a man, she'd stay working. The future was too uncertain to trust in a man who had no prospects. Who, instead of saving his money, spent money on frivolous holidays, on self-indulgent fun. Such a man as her father had been was not for her.

She told herself this over and over, but she still yearned for Tell Hardin.

'Are you seeing him again?' Beverley asked, her head cocked in interest.

'Who?' Molly blinked at her. Did she mean Tell?

'Luis, my dear.'

'Oh, no, I don't think so. He's going to Mexico City today, and may not be back here in Acapulco for a long time. I wasn't sure how much longer we'd be here.'

'Another several weeks, I'm sure. We're about halfway through the first draft. I'll finish that and then we can see about heading for another location. I should check in at home, see how things are going there. Then maybe we could travel up to Canada, stay in Banff. I have friends there, too.'

'I believe you have friends all over,' Molly said.

'Just places I've stayed for a while. I do like meeting new people and seeing new places. I think you have to live in a place a while to get the feel of it, don't you?'

Molly nodded, but wondered how authentic the feel of Mexico was living in a luxurious hotel. A flat in town would be more authentic. Not that she would trade staying here for anything. It was wonderful.

It was wonderful, but there was still work to be done. Molly worked all day, Beverley showing no signs of flagging. She took a couple of breaks to swim and lie in the sun briefly, wondering where else a secretary could take breaks in a pool. She surely had the best job in the world.

In the evening, she was still at the computer, trying to catch up with Beverley's dictation. The woman could go on and on, and Molly was hard pressed to keep up. It didn't look as if Beverley was reaching another period where she couldn't work. And of course Molly wanted another day. A day to ride with Tell.

The time passed slowly. Day after day, Beverley dictated, Molly transcribed. And dreamed of Tell. He didn't come round and Molly didn't contact Miguel. There was no message to pass on, and she still didn't know when she would have a day free.

She wondered what he was doing during the time she didn't see him. Had he found another girl on holiday, one who was out for a good time and didn't care if he didn't have any money? Or were things so tight that he couldn't afford much and was saving until

such time they could be together, so that he could pay
his way? He'd seemed determined on that the day
they'd gone sightseeing. Molly smiled remembering
their afternoon, and the meal at his camp. She smiled
a lot in remembering things about Tell. She wished
he were . . .

Back to typing. No use dreaming dreams that would
never be. She'd learned that in her childhood.

At last the day she'd been waiting for arrived.
Beverley walked into her room in the afternoon and
dropped a tape on the desk.

'That's it. I'm exhausted, totally dried up. I can't
write another word until I recharge my batteries. I
don't want anyone to even mention Black Jack
Pershing to me. I want to forget I ever knew about
the damn man!' She ran her hands through her short
hair.

Molly's heart leaped; she'd have her day with Tell
after all, and soon. She could finish what she had and
the tape on the table tonight. Tomorrow she'd be free.

'I thought I'd drive up to Taxco and see the silver
they have up there; they're famous for it, you know.
Do you want to come with me?' Beverley invited.

'I was thinking of going riding on the beach on my
next day off,' Molly said tentatively.

'Good idea. I haven't done that in ages. Maybe I'll
go with you. It's no fun to do things by yourself all
the time. Though you haven't complained once.
Priscilla used to complain all the time that there was
no one around to do things with. But you don't,
Molly; you do your job well and find entertainment
for yourself when we're not working. It's refreshing.
Riding sounds fun. I was raised on a ranch, you
know.'

Molly held her breath. She was pleased Beverley liked her performance, but she didn't want Beverley to go riding; she wanted to go with Tell. But she couldn't tell Beverley that without answering a lot of questions about the man. Beverley had warned her off him; what would she say if she discovered Molly was seeing him? She might not be so pleased about that.

Beverley fell silent for a moment, gazing out over the view. 'No, I think I'll keep to my original plan, and go to Taxco. Are you sure you don't want to come?'

Molly let her breath out slowly, unaware that she'd been holding it. She smiled and shook her head.

'Thanks, but I think I'll just stay around here.' She was anxious to see Miguel, let him send a message that she would have time to ride. He was her only way to contact Tell.

'I'm sorry Luis had to leave for Mexico City; he could have shown you around. His family has lived here for years as well as having a lovely home in Mexico City. He's quite a catch.' Beverley smiled slyly at Molly, her bright eyes twinkling in excitement.

'I'm really not looking for a catch,' Molly said slowly, her eyes on her computer. 'He's very nice . . .'

'But doesn't excite you. Well, there'll be other men. I know lots.'

'Now, Beverley, you're not trying to tie me up with anyone, are you? You'd lose another secretary if you did that.'

'You're right. Perish the thought. I like the work you do, Molly. Stay away from all men!' Beverley laughed and patted Molly on the shoulder. She drifted from the room, and Molly began typing frantically.

How long before she could take a walk and talk to Miguel? How could she casually leave and not have Beverley suspect anything? Would she? Or was Molly just self-conscious because of her guilty conscience?

Guilty conscience? She'd done nothing to feel guilty about. Beverley had suggested she stay away from Tell, but only because he was trouble. She was only seeing him to pass the time when she had it free. He meant nothing beyond that.

What about the other evening? Had Beverley not arrived when she did, Tell would have been considerably more than just a casual friend to while away her free time.

Molly's cheeks burned in remembrance, and her heart sped up. His kisses were intoxicating, his very touch seared her skin, made rational thought impossible. But the other night had surely been madness, not to be repeated.

The hours dragged by slowly as each moment Molly longed to fly to Miguel and have him contact Tell. But she diligently transcribed the tapes Beverley had dictated. It was late afternoon before she'd allow herself the break she'd been longing for.

Casually she stretched and moved to the patio. Beverley was not in sight. Molly didn't wait.

She was disappointed when she found that Miguel was not on duty. A young man named Carlos was behind the desk.

'Miguel will be on again tomorrow,' he told her.

'Oh, but he is to give a message to someone for me. Will he be around later today?'

'No, *señorita*, today is his day off. He will not be back until morning.'

Molly's heart sank. She nodded, and turned away, tears threatening. She'd so counted on having Miguel contact Tell; she'd never thought he might not be here. And she couldn't remember where Tell's camp was. Would it do any good to go into Acapulco and see if he was on the beach there? No, there would be thousands of people on the beach—she'd never find one tall, ruggedly handsome man among all the sunbathers.

She'd have to wait until tomorrow. Disappointment swept through her. She'd been so counting on seeing him, on riding with him once Beverley had told her she wouldn't be working on the morrow. What if Beverley was ready to work again the following day, and Tell didn't come?

The evening was long and lonely for Molly. She finished transcribing all the tapes, double-checked some of her work and sat out on the balcony well into the night. She hoped Tell would come, as he had before, but he did not.

As soon as Beverley left the next morning for her trip to Taxco, Molly walked down to the concierge's desk. Miguel was on duty and she asked him to contact Tell for her. Returning to her room, Molly opened her sliding door to make sure she didn't miss Tell's arrival, if he came. She dressed quickly in her bikini, planning to sunbathe to while the hours away. With anticipation rising, she lay on the lounger beside the pool. How long before he came?

The morning passed. The sun reached its zenith. Molly moved to the shade offered by the umbrella, changing her chair so that she could gaze over the sparkling waters of Acapulco Bay. The spanking white of the cruise ship drawing into the harbour drew her eye. Its horns blew, joyfully announcing its arrival. Molly could imagine the excitement of the tourists as they lined the deck, eyes drinking in the beauty of the scene. In only moments, they would be flooding the gangplank, and spilling out into Acapulco to sample its beaches, shops, restaurants and, later, its nightlife.

For a moment, she envied them. She glanced again over her shoulder to the empty hillside. There was no sign of Tell. Had he got her message? Had he changed his mind about wanting to see her again? Was he not coming?

She closed her eyes and settled back on the lounger, concentrating on the warmth that reflected from the patio, the soft air that caressed her skin as she dozed in the shade. She could hear the murmur of the hotel workers in the background, the soft hum of the pool's filter. Soon she fell asleep.

It was mid-afternoon when Molly awoke. She looked again for Tell, disappointed when she didn't see him, but almost resigned now. She'd get something to eat and do something else for the rest of the afternoon, not just sit and wait for a man who obviously was not coming.

Beverley had taken the jeep, so Molly was without transport. She donned her cover-up and gathered a book and hat in her bag. Wandering down to the lobby, she planned to catch a ride to the beach club, where she could eat from the buffet, snorkel in the sheltered pools and read her book. She'd have people around her, even if she didn't want to talk to them. It was better than remaining in her room.

Miguel was on duty. Molly went to enquire about the shuttle service to the beach club.

'In only another ten minutes, *señorita*, the bus leaves. It returns every half-hour.'

'Thank you.' She hesitated, then asked, 'My message to Tell Hardin, did he get it?' She hated asking, but if he had received the message then there was something that prevented . . .

'Sí, *señorita*. It was delivered.'

She nodded and smiled politely at him, turning away to await the bus. She refused to speculate on why Tell hadn't come. Perhaps he no longer wanted to spend time with her.

Molly stayed at the club until it grew dark. She caught the bus back to the hotel, climbed the steep drive to her room, heading straight for the shower. When she was finished, she donned her nightgown and light robe. She had started a good mystery and it would occupy her through the evening. She was anxious to start it again.

Ordering a salad from room service, she moved to slide open her door for the nice breeze. Standing in the doorway, her eyes moved around the patio, disappointed again. Wait—on the table, a dark pile. She moved closer to see what it was, curiosity aroused.

Dark jeans were folded neatly on the table, and a white strip of paper showed beneath the folds. She picked them up and moved towards the light. Tell?

Had he just come by? Had she missed him after all?

The handwriting was bold, large.

Pick you up at ten tomorrow. In case you don't have jeans, wear these. Wear bathing suit, no shirt necessary. Tell

Excitement blossomed within Molly as a smile

threatened to split her face. He'd come after all. And he still wanted to see her tomorrow. At ten. She hugged the jeans against her chest, closing her eyes to better see his dear visage. She'd see him in person in the morning!

Molly tried on Tell's jeans. They were only slightly loose, though long. She was surprised; she'd thought they would be far too big on her, since he was so large. Carefully, she rolled up the legs so that she could walk without tripping. She stood before the mirror, startled at the image that was reflected. Jeans that followed the line of her hips, a narrow waist and full breasts in a revealing pink bikini-top. Her eyes sparkled, and her cheeks were rosy with the sun and excitement. No way was she going to meet Tell Hardin looking like this.

She reached for her shirt. Buttoning it up, she looked more like a young woman going out to ride a horse. She had no boots, of course, but did put on a pair of tennis shoes.

Molly was ready long before the appointed time and could scarcely sit still waiting for the minutes to drag by.

Promptly at ten, there was a knock on the door. Molly flew to answer it, a bright smile on her face.

Tell's dark, handsome face smiled down at her as she flung the door wide. His eyes ran over her, dancing with amusement.

'Didn't read all the note, huh?' he asked, reaching out to unfasten one button of her blouse.

'Tell.' Molly's hands captured his, stopping his movement, but not before he'd unfastened another button, his fingers burning where they brushed the tops of her breasts. She stepped back, away from his overwhelming presence.

'Molly.' He leaned over and brushed her lips lightly with his. 'I said no shirt necessary. I want to see you riding in the warm sun with only your bathing suit. You need the jeans for protection, but not the top.'

I do, too, she thought—protection from you.

'Ready?'

She nodded, and went back for her bag. She didn't know what to bring, but thought a towel and sunscreen would be needed.

Tell seated her in his little rental car and climbed in the driver's side. Checking around the car, he hit the steering-wheel.

'Damn! I left my wallet back at the camp.' His eyes met Molly's. 'Can you lend me some money until later? It'll take ages to drive back to camp now. I reserved the horses for eleven—we'd be late.'

She dropped her eyes, afraid he'd see the disappointment and hurt she felt reflected. Yet why should she feel that way? She'd known all along he was a drifting cowboy, with not even enough money to stay in a proper hotel. She could say no and leave. Or pay for the day, enjoy his company and part after having ridden on the beaches of Mexico.

'Sure, I have plenty,' she said softly, daring to look up to meet his eye.

'I'll pay you back.'

She shrugged and turned to the window.

No amount of wishing or dreaming would change anyone. Tell Hardin was who he was. One of the things that attracted Molly to Tell was his attitude towards life. If he chose to be free, do what he wanted and not worry about stability and security, she couldn't change him. She didn't really want to. She wished she could be more like him.

A day on the beach didn't make a lifetime commitment. She'd enjoy the time, the company and the event. A memory to cherish down the years.

'I'm looking forward to this,' she confided as they reached the main road, turning away from Acapulco, towards the airport, towards the wilder open beaches of the Pacific.

'I'm glad; I am too. Your boss let you off again, eh?'

'She's hit a writer's block again, and gone off to see the silver at Taxco. She left yesterday.' Molly didn't say she'd been free all day; he must know that. She was suddenly shy with Tell, not wanting him to feel sorry for her for spending the day alone, waiting for him.

'Didn't she invite you?'

'Yes, but I . . .' Too late Molly saw the trap. She didn't want him to know she'd forgone the trip to be with him.

'You what?'

'I . . . I thought riding might be fun.'

He chuckled and reached over to take her hand in his.

'Molly, is it so hard to say you wanted to spend some time with me?'

She nodded, refusing to look his way.

'Why?' he asked softly.

'I shouldn't,' she whispered.

'I like spending time with you,' he said easily.

'But it will be so hard to say goodbye.' She tried not to think about it.

'So we won't.'

'Tell, this is holiday time. Acapulco is a dream time. This isn't like real life. You're on vacation, and I'm not working at a regular job. It will end. You'll leave, I'll leave and it will be goodbye.'

'I'll come see you in LA.'

She giggled, picturing him in his faded cut-offs riding an old horse down the LA freeways.

'I don't think they have many ranches in LA.'

'So come visit me in Texas.'

She turned to look at him in surprise. 'Do you have a place in Texas? I thought cowboys stayed in bunkhouses.'

'I have a bed; you can share that with me,' he said audaciously, slanting a look down at her.

Colour stained her cheeks and she held his look as long as she could before dropping her gaze. Her heart pounded beneath her shirt, the images of them together danced before her eyes.

'Would we be the only two in the bunkhouse?' she asked.

Tell roared with laughter, his hand tightening on hers. Molly smiled; his laughter was infectious. The whole thing was absurd, but fun to dream about.

'Ah, Molly, love, what shall I do about you?' His face sobered, his tone grew pensive. 'What shall I do?'

Tell's attention was on driving. The road dipped over the crest of the hills encircling Acapulco Bay and dropped down to run near the sea. Lush palms towered along the road, the dense shrubbery and green plants making a barrier to the view of the Pacific that lurked beyond the road.

Silently they drove on until at last Tell turned into the drive of the Revolcadero beach. Towering on either side of the drive were two of the luxury hotels that pampered the rich and famous. The Acapulco Princess rose like an Aztec pyramid ten storeys above the beach, to the left the Pierre Marques, low and rambling. Tell drove past and on to the beach, turning towards the south. Before long he stopped. To the land side, a corral of horses and an open stable, to the sea a magnificent white sandy beach, stretching south as far as Molly could see.

'Thought we could ride south, have a picnic lunch, swim and then come back,' Tell said as he parked the car.

'Sounds wonderful. I brought a towel, and I have my suit on.'

'And a shirt you don't need,' he grumbled.

She smiled. 'But it will keep the sun off me, so I don't burn.'

'You've gotten a good tan since you've been here. I don't think you'd burn.' He reached out to draw a finger down her cheek, follow along her jawline, drop lower, down her neck, to the edge of the shirt, trace the edge.

'Stop it. I want to go riding.' She snatched his finger away and turned to open her door.

'Me, too,' he said softly. 'Me, too.'

CHAPTER NINE

TELL drew saddlebags from the back of the little rental car, and smiled at Molly.

'I remembered the other stuff, anyway. I had a lunch fixed for us, and the drinks are wrapped in towels to stay cool. Ready?'

She nodded, her bag in hand. Following him to the stables, she watched the way he moved effortlessly over the uneven ground. His jeans were low-slung, his shirt open, swinging back in the movement of his body. He wore old scuffed tennis shoes, but they looked out of place. She could picture him in boots with a stetson hat shading his face from the sun.

Tell waited for her at the entrance, taking her arm in his hand and propelling her through the large airy stable to the back office.

'How well can you ride?' he asked.

'I'm not great, but I can stay on a horse.'

Tell relayed their abilities to the man in the office and before long one of the stable boys brought out two horses, tying them in the cross ties, and turning to bring out the saddles.

'You saddle your own?' Tell asked, handing her the saddlebags.

'I guess I could.' She looked dubious.

'I'll do them.'

Molly stepped back out of the way and watched Tell saddle the horses. Like everything else he did, he made it look easy. In no time both were ready to ride.

He tied the saddlebags on his mount, the hold-all on the smaller horse that Molly would ride.

Leading them outside, he drew up.

'Up you go. I'll double-check your stirrups.'

Molly mounted, the horse standing docilely as Tell checked the length of the stirrups.

'Too long. Move your leg, I'll shorten it.' He handed her the reins of both horses, and moved to shorten the stirrup on her left side. Sliding his hand along the outside of her leg, he steered her foot into the stirrup. Molly felt the warmth of his touch through the thick cotton of the jeans, her skin tingling in awareness. She swallowed hard.

Tell moved to the other side, adjusted the stirrup and slid his hand along her leg between the saddle and her thigh. This time, he rubbed her leg softly, his fingers hot through the thick material, the tremors his touch caused threatening to engulf her. Slowly his hand moved upwards, and Molly stared at him through wide eyes. Her stomach was molten lava, her heart skipped a beat, and desire for him rose and threatened to drown her. Afraid of her own feelings, she snatched at his hand and drew it away.

'You fill out these jeans better than I do,' he said, squinting up at her in the sun.

Molly was lost in the thin sliver glint staring back at her. She was conscious of his touch, the heat searing through her, the restless stamp of the horses' hoofs, and the muffled roar of the surf. It was a moment in time she'd never forget.

Tell took his reins and mounted, leading the way slowly down towards the water's edge. On firmer sand, the horses seem eager to go, and he started off at a trot, Molly keeping pace with him. Soon they increased to a canter and splashed in the water the receding waves deposited.

The sun shone from a cloudless sky; the water to their right was blue and clear, the waves breaking with regularity on the pristine sand. The spray kicked up by the horses evolved into millions of rainbow-glistening drops, showering the riders, the horses, until everything was wet.

On and on they rode, past sunbathers, surfers, other riders whose horses were tethered on the shore. On and on across the endless beach Tell and Molly rode. Molly never wanted to stop. She could ride until they reached the South Pole. The beach beckoned, the horses were fresh and she rode in happiness. The day was glorious. She didn't want anything to mar its perfection.

Tell drew up, slowing the horses to a walk. As they blew gently, and splashed in the water, Tell grinned at Molly. He looked younger, carefree, happy. And as if he were born to ride horses. He looked as if he were a part of the animal, moving with him, sitting as a part of the horse, not separate as a rider. Molly smiled at the picture.

She was smiling a lot today. Happiness bubbled just beneath the surface, and it was all she could do to contain it within her, having forgotten for the moment that it was her money paying for the rides.

'Want to stop? Swim a little, then eat?'

'Or we could keep riding forever,' she said, still gazing longingly southwards.

'It'd get cold about Chile,' he said drily, pulling his mount to a stop.

'You're so practical.'

'You don't usually accuse me of that.' He dismounted, reaching up to lift Molly down. 'But you are always accusing me of something.'

'That's not true.' She tried to remember; *did* she always accuse him of something?

'And arguing with me. If I suggest something, you always have another answer. You can't agree with me on anything.'

'That's not true.'

He smiled at her. 'It is. If I say the ocean is blue . . .'

She looked over to the sea. It was blue, a turquoise, teal-colour blue. 'Well, to be strictly accurate, it's more aqua or teal than a real blue blue.'

He swatted her gently on the bottom. 'See what I mean? Nothing I say gets a simple "yes, I agree".'

Molly looked at him from under her lashes. 'If you were to say you were a drifting cowboy who can charm the birds from the trees, I might agree.' She met his gaze bravely, though she could scarcely believe she'd been so bold.

He looked down into her blue eyes, the amusement in his fading, the grey growing smoky. She took a deep breath, the air charged with tension.

'You'd still not agree. Anyway, it's not true. Tell me why you wore this shirt.'

Molly stood still as his fingers unfastened the buttons one by one. By sheer will-power, the trembling she felt inside she kept inside, even when it threatened to take charge. She would not let him know how his touch affected her.

Slowly he drew the shirt from her shoulders, down her arms, his hands skimming her silky skin, dropping it carelessly on the sand.

She refused to meet his eyes, staring fixedly on the strong brown column of his throat.

'Well?'

She swallowed; it was awkward to talk about it. He was so open and carefree; she was too reserved to just go about practically unclothed.

'It seemed too...too...sexy,' she ended in a whisper.

Tell chuckled softly, his finger beneath her chin, tilting her head to meet his gaze.

'Honey, you *are* sexy, sexy as hell. You have the figure a man longs for, curves in the right places, long legs for your pint size. Your eyes are beautiful. And you tantalise a man with the austere glasses you wear. Take them off...'

He eased them from her face and carefully folded them, slipping them into her nerveless hand.

'With glasses you try to look like the prim young miss you long to be, with them off, however, you're one beautiful, free, sexy lady.' His head blotted out the sky as his mouth gently brushed against hers.

Molly closed her eyes and stood before him, longing for more. He didn't fail her. His lips brushed again, then claimed hers in a kiss that was all-consuming. Tell's arms went around her and she was crushed to his warm chest, his lips moved against hers and Molly moved in return, opening her lips, offering Tell what he wanted, what she wanted.

Her glasses slipped from numb fingers and fell softly on the white sand as her hand moved against his skin, beneath his opened shirt, feeling the strong muscles ripple against her touch as she moved closer. Her lips moved against his, her tongue duelled with his, the blood pounded in her heart, in her ears, through her body as his touch aroused her as never before. Hot, wild, searing, the kiss went on and on.

Molly moved against Tell, her skin fevered by his touch, moving against his strong chest, only the thin fabric of her bikini-top separating them. She longed for it to disappear, longed to feel his body against hers, feeling the pleasure she knew he would give her.

Breathing ragged, rational thought beyond her, Molly could only feel. Feel the ecstasy Tell's mouth wrought, feel the electric pulse between them, feel the strong beat of his heart against her breasts, feel the heat of the sun matched by the fiery sensation threatening to consume her.

Molly didn't feel the strings of her bikini-top unfasten. She could only feel the delights Tell's hands evoked, tracing lines of fire and enchantment along her back, feeding the growing flame within her, strengthening her, weakening her, overwhelming her.

When he moved, she gasped with the shock of his hand on her breast, his callused palm taking the weight of it as his thumb slowly traced the rosy tip. Molly broke the kiss and stared up at him with wide, startled eyes.

Tell's eyes were a deep smoky grey as he gazed back down at her, taking in her tousled hair, her swollen lips, dropping his gaze lower to see her milky white skin revealed by the lowered top. Slowly he lowered his head and gently took the nipple he'd been caressing into his mouth.

'Oh, God!' Molly moaned, closing her eyes as the exquisite delight flooded her body. She'd never had a man touch her like this before, never felt a man's lips on her breasts. An unexpected surge of pure pleasure coursed through her, a fiery flame that licked deep within her being. Her hands clutched his shoulders, moved to thread themselves into the thick head of hair, holding him against her as she swayed with the bliss that filled her.

She felt the zip of the jeans lower, his warm fingers against her skin.

'No. Oh, Tell, please stop, I can't.' Panic engulfed her as she pushed against him. She couldn't let herself be taken on the beach in broad daylight. She couldn't let a drifting cowboy upset her so that all her standards were relaxed.

He straightened, holding her around the hips, his breathing erratic and hard. For a long moment he stared at her, almost in anger.

Molly blinked up at him, slowly drawing up her bikini-top. Her eyes filled with tears. She didn't want to hurt him, or make him angry, but she needed time. She needed space from this disturbing man.

Tell's face forcibly relaxed and he kissed her cheek, moving abruptly towards the horses. 'You're right. It's not the time or the place. I'll tether the horses and we can go swimming.'

Molly watched him lead the horses up the sand towards some sparse grass. Perversely disappointed that he gave up so easily, even though she had insisted, she turned to the sea, refastening her top, and slipping out of the jeans. She'd plunge into the cool sea and hope it could quench the fire that burned deep within her for Tell Hardin.

She walked to the water's edge and hesitated. The waves looked bigger here than on Acapulco Bay beaches. The frothy water washed around her ankles. Dared she dive into the waves?

Tell joined her at water's edge. She glanced at him then quickly back to the water. He was wearing a brief swimsuit, the tell-tale bulge the only sign of their recent kiss. More than kiss. Heat rose again in Molly's cheeks and she could feel the increased rate of her heart. Would he see?

'The surf here is strong; can you swim in it?' Tell asked.

She nodded, afraid to trust her voice.

'We could always go skinny-dipping,' he suggested, his voice low, amused.

She turned to find him laughing at her as the words of protest died on her lips.

'No, I thought not, Miss Prim and Proper. Come on.'

Taking her hand, he moved into the cool Pacific. Diving together through an incoming wave, they passed the crest and swam in the calm behind. Molly enjoyed herself. The water was refreshing without being cold. The swells that lifted them then ran on past to crash against the beach added to the enjoyment. When she was tired, she lay on her back and floated. Tell swam near by, diving from time to time and staying down a long time. Molly wished she could hold her breath for as long.

'Ready to go back?' He was some yards away.

She rolled over to tread water. 'Yes; time for lunch?'

'I'm hungry, how about you?'

'Famished.' She began swimming towards the shore.

In only a couple of strokes, Tell was beside her, lazily paddling alongside her as they moved with the swells.

'We can catch a wave and body-surf on in,' he suggested.

'I'm willing to try, anyway,' she replied, glancing over her shoulder to see the next swell.

Tell reached for her hand and strongly propelled them to the crest of the next wave. As it broke, they glided in on the frothy, churning white water, coming to a rest on the soft sand. Water drained from around them and Tell stood up, pulling Molly up before the next wave washed around them.

'That was fun!' she exclaimed, happiness blooming again.

He watched her as she brushed some of the water off, slicked back her hair. For a moment, Molly thought he might kiss her again. But he said only, 'Let's eat.'

Tell had provided an excellent lunch—chicken, crisps, fruits and cold drinks. The towel insulator had kept everything cool. They ate and watched the soothing rhythm of the surf, crashing over and over on the sandy bank, receding to crash again. Molly became almost mesmerised by it, its soothing sound, regular beat and fascinating spray of colours a quiet beauty to lose oneself in.

'A penny for your thoughts.' Tell broke into her dreaming.

'Oh, I was just thinking how perfect today is.' She turned to look at him, smiling at the picture he made. Brown and muscular, he was lying on a towel, his head propped by one arm, his eyes closed. Molly remembered their first day at the beach in Acapulco. She'd studied him then; she had a chance to now. He was so very special. How could she bear it when they must part?

'So tell me more about Miss Molly Spencer,' Tell invited drowsily.

Molly lay back on her towel, closing her eyes against the bright sun. The air was warm, a gentle breeze blew in from the water, and the only sound she could hear was the muffled surf.

'Like what?'

'How you happened on the kind of work you do, where you went to school, what you're going to do when you marry your rich husband.'

'I never said I wanted to marry a rich man, only one who was comfortably off. My parents were dirt-poor. I would never wish that on anyone.'

'Did it ever occur to you that you might fall in love with someone who didn't have money? As your parents must have done?'

She was silent for a moment, fighting against the knowledge that refused to be hidden any longer. *She loved Tell Hardin*. She had fallen for a man who had nothing, just like her mother. But she would not repeat her mother's mistake. She would look for security. If she could find it with love, so much the better. If not, security would be lasting.

'Did you fall asleep?' Tell asked.

'No, I . . . I won't fall for someone who is poor. I couldn't live like that all my life.' She was trying to explain to him, to herself. She couldn't bear the thought of raising children the way she'd been raised. She wanted more for her children.

'Money's not everything, Molly.'

'I know. But for me it represents a lot. It may be different for you, Tell. You're strong. You can make it doing whatever you want. And you're satisfied. But it's different for me.'

'I think you're strong.'

She rolled her head over to look at him. He was still lying back with his eyes closed, his chest rising and falling, tantalising her fingers.

'I'm not strong,' she whispered, looking away. 'I'm so afraid sometimes.'

'Hell, everyone's afraid sometimes.'

'Even you?'

He laughed, 'Even me. What has your little mind invented for me—Superman?'

'No, but you never seem to care much for what others think, or care about. You seem so self-sufficient, so confident.'

'I am confident in myself, and in things I do.'

'Well, I'm not,' she said.

'You should be; you've got talents, skills, experience. Be confident in them. You would never be destitute; you could always care for yourself and anyone else who depended upon you. I don't know what your mother was like, but I'm beginning to know you.'

Molly lay quiet. It was easy for him to say; he didn't suffer from feelings of inadequacy, fear of deprivation.

'Do you ride in rodeos?' she said, to change the subject. She didn't want talk about her past any more. She thought all cowboys were in rodeos, and could easily imagine Tell on a bucking horse, taming him.

'Change of subject, huh? I used to. I'm too old now. I'm thirty-two. You need to be a young man to ride the rodeo circuit.'

'Tell me about it,' she invited.

And so he did. Told her about riding rodeos, and ranching in Texas, and more stories of his brothers and sisters and cousins. Molly loved listening to him talk. His voice was a pure delight to listen to, his tales funny, heart-warming and so foreign to the girl who had been alone most of her life.

Tell asked more questions of her own life and slowly she revealed some things she'd never thought she'd talk about. And found the hurt she'd expected had eased—the memories weren't as painful as they once had been. But the resolve was as strong. She'd never run the risk of any children of hers having a similar childhood.

It was a wonderful afternoon and she was sorry when he suggested they begin their ride back.

'It's not that late,' she protested.

'But I want to take you on the dinner cruise on the bay tonight, and you have to get back in time to change for that,' he said.

Her eyes lit up and her smile brightened her whole face. She'd longed to go on the dinner cruise, never thinking she'd get the chance. And not with Tell. For a moment, she paused. Was she to pay for the event as well? Well, and if so, so be it. She'd still get to spend some more time with him. Tomorrow she could be back at work.

She pulled on his jeans, aware as she hadn't been that morning that these jeans had covered Tell's body, had rubbed against his skin in the same way they encased hers. Zipping them shut, she looked around for her shirt. Shaking out her towel, she rolled it up and stuffed it into her bag. She still didn't see her shirt.

Tell had his saddlebags tied on his horse and had donned his jeans. He wore no shirt and she watched him as, leading the horses, he came up beside her. His skin was bronzed, his walk arrogant and damn-all, his dark hair tossed in the afternoon breeze. He was gorgeous!

'Ready?'

'Tell, have you seen my shirt?' She should be looking for that, not at him.

'Yep.'

'Where is it?'

'Packed away. I told you I didn't want you to wear a shirt.'

She glanced down at her brief bikini-top, the snug jeans below.

'I can't ride home like this,' she protested.

'Sure you can.'

One finger came out and traced the edge of the jeans. Molly's stomach jerked from the contact, her heart beat wildly.

'Tell . . .'

'Come on, sweetheart, pamper me.'

His finger moved again, trailing fire along the edge of her bikini top. Molly jumped back as if stung. She had better get away from him while her limbs would still obey her command. She felt as if her legs would melt beneath her. Could she manage the few steps to the horse, get back on?

She managed, barely. Gathering the reins, she turned in the direction of home, kicking her horse. Cantering through the shallow waves, the water splashing up around her, Molly laughed with the sheer pleasure of the day. Behind her she could hear the pounding of Tell's horse as he rode to overtake her. Pursued by the man she loved, for a moment, she was happy.

She urged her mount faster, but Tell's horse was superior and he soon overtook her. Keeping the furious pace for several minutes, gradually they slowed, Molly feeling safer on horseback than on the sand with Tell. The look he gave promised retribution.

When they reached the stables, the buildings were deserted, the Mexicans at siesta. Tell led the horses inside and stripped them of their saddles, turning them out into the corral. Walking back into the dark interior of the stable, he saw Molly rummaging in his saddlebags, looking for her shirt.

'Uh-huh, I like you like you are.' He reached for the saddlebags.

She hung on, trying to find her shirt, laughing at his attempt to draw the saddlebags from her. He was teasing her, she knew it, because he could easily take them away if he wanted.

'Tell, I need my shirt.'

'No.' He pulled again, spinning her around the floor of the stable.

Molly laughed again. 'Tell, stop.'

'OK.' He dropped the bags, and moved to her, pushing her back against the stable wall, moving in to kiss her with hard lips, softening only when they touched her. He pushed the bags out of the way, his body pressed in against hers, and Molly was lost . . .

Lost to the hardness of the wall behind her, to the sweet smell of hay, the dimness of the light, the heat of the afternoon. She could only feel Tell's mouth against hers, his strong body pressing against her, his tongue plunging in to taste her, give her a taste of him. On and on the kiss went and Molly thought she was floating to heaven. The day was hot, and so was the blood pounding through her body. His skin seared her where he touched and his mouth was an endless source of erotic excitement. When he moved to nibble at her earlobe, Molly almost sank to the ground, only the hardness of his body pushing her against the rough stable wall keeping her upright. The solid wall of his chest crushed her breasts and she revelled in the sensations he evoked. His long, hard legs captured hers, while his fingers threaded themselves into her hair, positioning her mouth where he wanted it.

'Pardon, *señor*.'

The gentle Spanish voice broke the spell. Tell stepped back slowly and tapped her lips with his finger. His eyes were smoky as he stared at her swollen lips, his finger tracing lightly.

'Sorry, *señor*. Thank you for returning the horses. They were good?'

'They were fine.' With a sigh, Tell straightened completely and turned to the old man.

Molly moved on shaky legs out into the bright sun as Tell crossed the stable to talk to the man. Slowly she walked to the car, thoughts of her shirt forgotten. What was she to do?

Her heart pounded at the lovemaking they'd shared. It had ended too soon. She loved Tell, ached with loving him, but dared not let him know. How he'd laugh at her. First because he wasn't rich, as she'd said a man would have to be, and second because he'd never given her any indication he wanted anything more than a holiday fling, someone to pass the time with while he holidayed in Acapulco.

It would all end soon. This was a fairy-tale existence, not real. And when it ended, as it had to, he'd go back to Texas and she'd go back to LA. Their lives were too different. Sadness welled up where happiness had been.

Tell joined her in the car and drove to the hotel.

'I'll pick you up at seven-thirty. The cruise starts at eight. Wear that pretty dress you had on the other night.'

Molly looked over at him, a hint of a smile in her glance. The magic wasn't over yet. There was still to-night and all the tomorrows that he was here. She would store up the memories to treasure down the years ahead. Smiling at him, she nodded, glad he'd see her in the pretty dress one more time.

When they pulled up before the *casita* that was Molly's, they saw the blue and white jeep parked before it. Beverley was back.

Molly's heart sank. Was this the end to the night's plans? Could she still go out with Tell, or would Beverley be ready to work again? Molly was afraid to find out. She wanted to go on the cruise!

Tell stopped the car, and reached in the back for her bag. Walking around the car to open her door, he glanced at the jeep.

'Boss back?'

'Looks like it. I don't know if this will change things.'

'It won't. If she asks you to do any work, tell her you'll have to do it in the morning—you have plans tonight. She'd not expect you to change them.'

'Maybe.' Molly wasn't convinced. If she were going with Luis, Beverley would be delighted. But Molly had already been warned against Tell. Beverley would be no support there.

'I'll be here at seven-thirty.' He kissed her cheek and slammed the door, watching as Molly walked away.

She paused at the door, and smiled shyly. 'I'll be ready.'

CHAPTER TEN

MOLLY let herself into her room quietly. If Beverley was sleeping or busy writing, Molly didn't want to alert her that she was home. She moved to the sliding glass door and looked out. No sign of Beverley on the patio, no light spilling from her room.

Closing the curtains, Molly began to get ready for the evening ahead. Laying her dress on the bed, she checked to make sure the repairs didn't show. She wanted to look her best for Tell.

Stepping beneath the warm shower, feeling the soothing water wash away the salt and sand from the day's outing, Molly remembered Tell's kiss on the beach. The feel of his mouth against hers, against her breast. The rapture she felt in his arms. Then she remembered the kisses from the other night. Had Beverley not interrupted, where would she be today? Would she have said no on the beach? Would she know the full love in her heart was shared by him? Or was she only a conquest during the holiday, forgotten once he'd gone?

Drying off, she determined that she would enjoy the evening and not think of the future, not consider what might have been. She knew where she was headed and couldn't, dared not, deviate from her chosen course. To do so would court disaster such as her mother had faced. But, knowing that, she could still spend time with Tell, enjoy herself, knowing it would not last. She could manage that much.

It had been inevitable once she'd turned on the shower that Beverley would know she was back. Soon after she donned her dress, she heard the soft tap at her sliding glass door. Drawing open the curtains, Molly opened the door.

'Hello, dear. Back, I see. Oh, you're dressing— going out?'

'Yes. I've been invited to the dinner cruise. Did you need me?' Molly held her breath. Please don't let anything spoil the night. She hadn't realised how much she was looking forward to the evening until she saw Beverley. She longed to feel Tell's arms about her as they danced, to feel the length of his body against hers as they swayed to music. She wanted just this one night, and prayed that nothing would spoil it.

'Oh, no. You go on and have a good time. You look very nice. I didn't realise Luis was back. Did you enjoy your days off? I had such fun in Taxco, bought more silver than I should have, but I do love shopping there. Come by later and I'll show you all my treasures. Maybe Luis would like to see them, too?'

Before Molly could answer, Beverley patted her on the arm. 'Don't let me keep you from finishing. I know you want to look your best. Just pop by if you have time. If not, tomorrow will do. I feel energised again. Think I'll dictate some tapes tonight. We'll be going full blast tomorrow. Have fun.'

Beverley smiled and strolled out to the patio, walking near the railing. Molly breathed a sigh of relief and turned to apply her make-up sparingly. The tan of the tropical sun gave her all the colour she needed. A touch of mascara and she was ready.

She debated wearing her glasses, warmed by the comments Tell had made on the beach, but in the end decided to leave them behind. She wanted to look glamorous for Tell tonight and to her mind glasses did not foster that at all.

She was ready long before seven-thirty. Each minute dragged by endlessly. She longed for Tell to arrive, yet dreaded the possibility of a meeting between him and her employer. Beverley was still on the patio. With luck, when Tell arrived, Molly could slip out and never have Beverley see who her escort for the evening was. Let her continue to think it was Luis.

Hearing the sound of his car, Molly grabbed her bag and let herself quietly out of the room. She quickly walked down the short walkway to the drive, anxious to get in the car and get away.

Tell arose on the far side of the car. He was dressed in tan trousers, a white shirt and navy blazer. To Molly's eyes, he looked very dressed up, and very handsome. For a moment she wondered how his clothes could look so nice with the limited means of camping.

'You look nice,' she blurted out, her heart swelling in anticipation of the evening ahead.

He smiled and came around the car. 'So do you.'

He held the door open for her and shut it carefully, as if she was precious cargo. For a wild, rough cowboy, he sure knew how to make her feel special.

Throwing a quick glance over her shoulder as they pulled away, Molly was reassured to see no sign of Beverley as they drove away. Breathing a sigh of relief, she turned back to the front.

'And what was that for?' Tell asked.

'What?'

'What? That sigh.'

'Oh, nothing. I'm glad we're going, that's all,' she told him.

'No trouble with your boss?'

'No.'

'Did she know you were going out?'

'Yes.'

Tell sighed and pulled to the side of the narrow road. 'What's up?' His narrow gaze pinned her to the seat of the car. She fidgeted beneath his gaze and looked away.

'Nothing.'

'Tell me,' he commanded.

'There's nothing to tell. Beverley thinks I'm going out with Luis Alverado.'

'Ashamed to be out with me, Molly?' His voice was silky, but the anger was not completely covered.

She faced him. 'No, of course not. Oh, Tell, I wouldn't ever want you to think that. It's just that Beverley told me that first day in Acapulco to stay away from you and I don't want to jeopardise my job. I told you that before.'

'Dammit, she wouldn't fire you for seeing me!'

'I don't want to take the chance.'

'So you'd rather lie?'

'No, I didn't lie. She thinks it's Luis, I just didn't correct her.'

'I must remember you're not so prim and proper when it suits you not to be.' His voice was still grim.

'Oh, Tell, don't be mad at me. I wanted this evening to be perfect.'

He turned to the front again, his hands gripping the wheel hard. For a moment, Molly wondered if he'd like to grip her neck that hard, but why he should be so angry was beyond her. She was not ashamed to be seen with him, only trying to keep away from a confrontation with her boss.

'Before I forget.' His voice was cold. He reached into his pocket and drew out several folded notes, handing them to Molly. 'I really only wanted a loan today. I forgot my wallet, though I know you thought I was cadging off you.'

She stared at the money, a feeling of guilt and shame invading her. She had thought that. Why hadn't she trusted him? Why couldn't she let go of the past and judge people on what they seemed? Why blame him for her father's lack?

'Thank you,' she said softly, reaching for the money. No wonder he was mad at her—all her actions did seem to point out that she was ashamed of him. And she wasn't. She enjoyed being with him; it made her happy and proud to be seen with him. How could she convey this to him?

She tucked the money in her purse as he put the car in gear and started up again. The ride was silent. Neither spoke as he negotiated the curves and hills leading down to Acapulco.

Molly was miserable. She'd so looked forward to their evening together; now it was spoiled and because of her. She should have believed him earlier, believed in him, that it was only a loan. She should have stood up to Beverley and told her about Tell. She was her own person—surely she was entitled to see whomever she liked in her free time. She should have stood up to Beverley before. Tell was probably right; she wouldn't be fired just for dating someone Beverley didn't like. Beverley liked her work; she would have put up with Molly's choice in companions.

Darting a quick glance at Tell, she turned back, disappointed and frustrated. She didn't want the evening to continue like this. It would be better to call it off.

'Tell.' She reached out her hand to touch him, resting it on his thigh. Instantly, his hand came to cover hers, moved it closer to him, resting on the warm muscles of his leg, his fingers tightening on hers. She caught her breath at the surge of emotion that engulfed her at his touch.

'Sometimes I could wring your neck, Molly Spencer. I can't figure you out. I think you like my company, and then you insult me. You seek me out with Miguel, and deny me to your boss. Lord, you make me angry!'

'I'm sorry. I didn't mean to. I do want to spend time with you, Tell. I...I like spending time with you. I'm sorry I didn't let Beverley know it was you I was going out with and say to hell with the consequences. Don't be mad. I want to enjoy tonight.'

He sighed and squeezed her hand again. He said nothing, but the tension between them seemed to fade away.

Parking the car near the wharfs, Tell threaded her fingers through his as he led the way to the sparkling white ship that cruised Acapulco Bay and short stretches into the Pacific. Across the dock was one of the luxury liners that stopped in Acapulco, its gleaming white sides towering over the dock, its lights illuminating the entire waterway. Festive, colourful flags fluttered in the evening breeze. There was an excitement in the air that was infectious. Molly's spirits rose.

Boarding the dinner ship, Molly was enchanted. It had a large dining area, its windows opened to the soft, scented air. Before and aft were large decks, small tables and chairs lining the rails. The decks were obviously for dancing.

Following the steward, Molly entered the dining-room and soon was seated at a table beside one of the large, open windows. The dining-room was full without being crowded. There was a small bar at one end. Despite the other people, Molly felt she and Tell were in a world of their own.

'This is perfect,' she said as she looked out of the window at the lights sparkling along the beaches of Acapulco. The water was calm and clear, reflecting the myriad lights from the rows of hotels lining the shore. Here and there in the large bay she could see the running lights of smaller boats, their owners also out to enjoy an evening on the water.

'I took the liberty of ordering for us earlier—I suppose you want to argue about that,' Tell said whimsically.

She looked at him and smiled. 'No, I don't. It sounds fine to me.'

He raised one eyebrow in mock astonishment and Molly felt her heart crash against her chest. Oh, heavens, if just looking at him caused this reaction, what would dancing with him do? She swallowed hard and looked back out of the window. Maybe coming here had been a mistake after all. But she could hardly wait.

As the ship pulled away from the harbour the stewards began serving dinner. The soft strains from the band floated in through the open windows. The song they were playing forever etched itself in Molly's memory as a part of Mexico.

The steward placed their plates before them. The medallions of veal and the fresh asparagus were delicious. Molly complimented Tell on his choice.

From then on they regained their former ease. Talking casually about the cruise, the sights from the ship, Tell pointed out Las Casitas D'Oro high on the distant hillside. The ship glided west, out to sea, then turned north to run along the coast for an hour or two before returning to port.

When they finished eating, Tell asked her to dance. Molly nodded, anticipation and anxiety warring. She longed to be in his arms again, but wondered if she could keep her secret safe. One touch from him set her emotions in a spin—could she dance with him all evening and not blurt out her love for him? Could she stand the gentle torment of touching him and not letting him know how much she loved him? How much she longed for him to touch her?

Tell led her to the aft deck. It was darker than the one on the bow, and less crowded. Sheltered from the breeze somewhat by the structure of the dining-room, it was warm and intimate. He drew her into his arms and began to move with the soft music.

His legs brushed against hers and sent shock waves of delight and yearning coursing through her body. His arms held her tightly against him; she could feel his heartbeat match her own.

Molly gave herself up to him, encircling his neck with her arms, pressing her breasts against his chest, moving her hips and legs as he dictated. The two of them moved as one.

One of his hands splayed against the bare skin of her back, holding her firmly against him. The other rested on her hips and moved as she moved, its heat penetrating the light material of her dress, burning her skin. Molly grew warmer. Perhaps they should be on the front deck; she needed the extra breeze to cool down.

Seduced by the touch of Tell, the romantic music and the floating euphoria of the cruise, she reached up and pulled his head down to her mouth. She wanted to feel his kiss, to dance in time with the dreamy music, lost in the rhapsody of Tell's touch, the feel of his lips and mouth on hers adding to the measure of fantasy she felt as the evening progressed.

His hands moved until they were on either side of her hips, moving her against him from side to side, slowly, sensuously, erotically. His mouth left hers to trail hot kisses along her cheek, her jaw, down her neck to the pulsating spot on her throat, back to her mouth.

Molly's legs were weak and trembling. She clung to Tell in a mist of desire and yearning. Her body clamoured for his, and she was impatient with the constraints between them, the limitations of the boat.

He broke off, and pulled her to the side, sitting in one of the chairs in the shadow of the engine-room.

'Much more of this and I'll ask the captain for a room. I want to talk to you.' His voice was ragged, his breathing erratic.

'Mmm.' She kissed him again, snuggling up against his strong chest, feeling his hands on her waist, caressing her through the flimsy soft material of her dress.

'Molly, I'm leaving, going back to Texas. My vacation is over.'

The words hit her like cold water. The feeling of euphoria and happiness ended as abruptly as if cut off. Coldness and fear struck her heart. Her voice was thick, and she could scarcely get the words out.

'Leaving?' She knew it would come. She had known it all along. But so soon?

'Yes. I do work, you know. Even though you think I'm some sort of bum. I have to get back to work.' He looked at her for a long moment. 'Come with me.'

She sat up, pushing away from him to sit on his legs. She was too disorientated to stand just yet. Trying to breathe, to feel something, she let his words echo over and over. Was her world ending? Trying to keep it light, she painted a smile on her face and faced him, but couldn't quite meet his eyes.

'To your bunkhouse? You never did say if it would be just the two of us.'

'I'm serious, Molly.'

'Me, too. Tell, I can't go with you.' There, she'd said it. Was that pain in her chest her heart breaking? She took a deep breath, trying to free the cold pain that was pressing down on her.

'Trust me, Molly. Trust me to care for you, look after you. Come with me!'

No words of love, none of marriage. How improper did he think she'd be? It was daring to share a cruise together, something quite different to go off to Texas together. What did he want? Just to continue their holiday romance? Was he realistic enough to know he couldn't afford to marry her, that they would end up like her parents? She knew he wanted her; every action he'd ever done had proved that. Was it the quest of the chase, satisfied when won?

'No, Tell, I can't go with you.' She stood up, moving to the railing, her legs working after all. The night was cold, or was it only her? She wished she'd brought a sweater. He followed her, swinging her round to face him.

'Why not? Because of money? If I were some rich bastard you'd come in an instant, wouldn't you? Women will do anything for money. Can't you trust me, Molly? Trust me to never let you be in want? Just come with me, as we are, and don't worry about the future.'

Sadly she shook her head, too afraid to take what he offered, too sure she knew where it would all lead—down a path she'd been as a child and didn't care to go again.

'No, Tell, I can't come with you. But thank you for asking me. I will always treasure that.'

Her voice broke on the last part and she turned away, blinking her eyes furiously. She would not cry before him.

For a long moment he said nothing, then in a strained voice he said softly, 'I'll miss you, Molly.'

It was almost more than she could stand.

'Could we dance again?' she asked, her voice tinged with sadness.

He drew her into his arms and moved back to the floor, swaying to the music, moving in time, but more like strangers, no longer close like before.

Molly felt encased in ice. She was numb to all feelings, except for where her body touched Tell. There she burned. He was leaving and she was staying. The wonderful meetings would be no more. No longer would she feel delightfully awful doing something not quite proper. No longer look forward to seeing him, learning something new, something different, as she had all along with this arrogant, forceful, dominating man.

The cruise became an endless nightmare. Molly wanted it to end, her anticipation of earlier only a cruel reminder of how much she had looked forward to the evening. Now she wanted to get off the boat, away from Tell, escape to the sanctuary of her own room. Had time stopped?

They danced, watched the shore as the boat returned to the bay, and disembarked with the others from the ship, the other people who had had a wonderful time, who were laughing and skipping around. Molly felt as if she were in a trance, soon to end. She hoped.

She spoke not a word as Tell whisked them through the city, up the hillside to her hotel. Pulling up before her door, he turned off the engine but made no moves beyond that.

Molly didn't want to move. To do so would end the evening, end her time with Tell forever. Yet it was already over. All over. Everything had changed.

He touched her lips gently with his finger. 'I want you, Molly! If you change your mind, leave a message with Miguel.'

'Goodnight, Tell.' She couldn't bring herself to say goodbye.

She yanked open her door and fled the car, not wanting him to touch her again lest she lose all control and give in to the longings of her heart.

Gaining the safety of her room, she leaned against her door, listening for the sound of the car, hearing it start, pull away. He was gone.

Molly burst into tears.

It was her own fault. She'd been playing with fire since that first night on the terrace. She should never have gone along with him, but he brought such excitement and novelty to her life. She was tired of the regimented life she'd set for herself. It had been such fun to do the unexpected with Tell.

He'd made her feel so alive, so daring. From buying that scandalous bikini, to their sexy rainy rendezvous at the supper at his camp, to the wild ride along the beach, he'd had her do things she'd never thought of before. Fun things, daring things, exciting things.

Fairy-tale kind of excitement.

She dressed for bed, and climbed under the sheets, tears flowing steadily. Curling up in a ball, she tried to ease the ache in her heart, the loneliness that was so overwhelming. Nothing worked. Crying softly in the night, Molly fell asleep.

She awoke the next morning with a raging headache. Donning her swimsuit, she went for a quick dip in the pool, the cool water refreshing, the invigorating exercise a balm to her battered nerves. She felt better for the swim and was able to greet Beverley pleasantly a short time later when they met for breakfast.

'Tell me about Taxco,' Molly urged, hoping to start her employer on a monologue to which she would have little need to contribute.

'It was wonderful. I went to the shops that actually beat the silver into thin strips before making the most exquisite jewellery.' Beverley launched into the details of her trip, capturing the nuances of the old city so well that Molly felt as if she had seen it in person. She listened to Beverley, focusing her attention on her every word to avoid thinking about Tell.

'Goodness, look at the time. I wanted to get an early start today.' Beverley glanced at her watch. 'And you haven't even told me how your days off were. How was the cruise?'

'Very nice.' Molly rose and moved around the pool, not wanting to talk about anything, but especially not last night. 'I'll get the computer turned on and collect the tape you did last night,' she said.

Throwing herself into her work, Molly sought to forget by sheer involvement. She transcribed each tape almost as soon as Beverley drew it from the recorder. Reviewing her transcriptions each night, she corrected any typos and misspellings. Staying up late until fatigue overcame her and she stumbled to bed was the only way she could get any sleep.

Despite her efforts, thoughts of Tell crept in. When was he leaving? Would he come by to see her one more time before going? Or was he waiting for some word from her before coming again? Should she send him a message from Miguel? Yet what could she say? Only goodbye.

Over and over she tried to imagine his life, working on a ranch, repairing fences, branding cattle. What else did he do? What did he do in the evenings? Would he now work late to avoid thinking of her? Or sit on a wooden porch and watch the evening come over the plains, sit with other cowboys and swap stories? Would he think of her, or would her memory fade after a few weeks?

She wished she could have gone with him, if only for a visit. Maybe seeing him in his setting would resolve things for her. At least she'd know in the future what kind of life he had, what his place looked like, what he did in his spare time. Now she'd always wonder. It made her heart ache.

Molly endured it for two days. The third morning when she awoke she resolved to send Tell a message. Miguel could get word to him. She'd see him once more. Maybe talk about coming to visit.

But of course, since she was in a hurry, Beverley was particularly demanding that morning. She wanted to verify several of the items she'd already incorporated in the book, forcing Molly to find the passages and read them back to her. After editing over and over, at last she was satisfied.

'That's all for today. I think I'll go to the beach club later; want to ride down with me?' she asked.

'I may.' Molly first wanted to get a message to Tell. Would he come this afternoon? Should she suggest he come tonight? How soon was he leaving? She suddenly wanted to see him again.

She hurried down to the lobby. Miguel's quiet smile greeted her when she entered the breezy expanse.

'*Buenos días, señorita.*'

'Hello, Miguel. I want to send a message to Señor Hardin.'

His face fell. 'But *señorita*, Señor Hardin, he is gone. His holidays ended and he is gone. Back to Texas.'

'I didn't know,' she said, her hopes sinking.

So, after all, he'd gone. Without a word of farewell, without seeing her again. Leave word with Miguel, he'd said. What for? So the next time he was down this way he'd learn that she'd changed her mind? When would he ever come to Acapulco again?

She walked listlessly back up the steep hill to the *casita*.

'Goodbye, Tell,' she said softly as the tears started again.

CHAPTER ELEVEN

TIME moved slowly. Molly no longer enjoyed the simple things that had brought her pleasure before. Everything reminded her of Tell. From the beauty of the view from her patio to swimming at the beach club, everything she did held memories. Was there a place in Acapulco she didn't associate with Tell?

Only the house of Luis Alverado. And she had no interest in renewing acquaintance with that nice young man. She'd rather do her job, then go for the long walks that had been her solace in the last few days.

She'd once wondered if she would ever tire of the view from her room, and she had not. But it caused her more pain than delight now. She remembered the first night she'd seen the stranger lurking in the shadows, how he'd frightened her at first, then intrigued her. He'd pointed out the hotels across the bay, and told her of the cruise ships.

Molly stood by the railing, looking out over the sunset, the sky shades of pink, mauve and purple. In the distance she saw one of the bright luxury cruise ships, and she could almost hear the music from it.

'Trust me, Molly. Trust me to care for you'. The words Tell had spoken echoed in her mind. She wished she could trust him, but, while he was young and fit now, what would the years bring? Would he ever want to marry her? Would he be killed young, like her father? Leaving her and a child, or, worse, *children*, to fend for themselves.

'You're strong'. She didn't feel strong. She felt afraid again. Afraid she'd lost something invaluable, yet afraid to trust someone as carefree as Tell. She *needed* stability and security in her life. She couldn't afford to gamble.

But she *was* strong; she had brought herself up from poverty to a nice standard of living. So maybe her fate was not that of her mother's. Maybe she could love a man, work with him to build a life together, one they could share until both were old. Maybe he would not die young, and leave her destitute.

'You've got talents, skills... you would never be destitute...' She could get a secretary's job anywhere; they were always in demand. She was a hard worker and good at her job. Beverley had complimented her several times, and she was a hard taskmaster.

'Trust me'. 'Trust me'. 'Trust me'. The words echoed over and over in her mind. Molly's eyes no longer saw the sunset and its glorious colours; she saw only Tell's dark face. She heard his voice, low and compelling, urging her to trust him, depend on him, count on him. He'd not let her down.

Could she do it?

What was the alternative? Endless years of the loneliness this last week had given her? Longing for the man she loved, wanting to be with him, wanting him to be with her? She'd made a mistake in saying no; could she correct it?

She loved him. She had to accept that. Could she trust him? Her heart would not let her do otherwise. The decision made, a great sense of peace invaded her.

She needed to talk to Tell, let him know she'd changed her mind, that she couldn't go on without him. She loved him, she wanted to be with him. Dammit, why did he have to be so far away when she made the most important decision of her life?

Slowly she walked back to her room. If she couldn't talk to him, maybe Miguel knew where she could mail a letter. She could write to him, see if he felt the same about wanting her to come.

And if he didn't?

The thought didn't bear thinking about.

Dear Tell. I'll come. I miss you too much to stay away. Trust me, you said. I do. I trust you with my life, my future, my heart. I love you, Tell. If you still want me to come, please let me know where. Love, Molly.

She re-read it; was it too forward? She smiled, imagining his teasing her about being so prim and proper. Was it proper to send such a letter? It was wildly improper from her point of view, but she was doing it. However improper, it was the only thing that might bring her happiness.

She put the letter in an envelope and walked down to the lobby. It was late, and the night clerk behind the desk told her Miguel was off duty, would not be back until the morrow. Could he help?

Reluctantly, Molly explained that she wanted an address from Miguel. The clerk took the envelope and wrote a note, leaving both on the desk for Miguel when he arrived the next morning.

'It will be taken care of, *señorita*.' He smiled at her, not at all struck by the oddness of the request.

Molly's heart felt lighter as she went to bed that night. Soon Tell would have the letter, soon she'd hear from him. She just had to!

Miguel called her the next morning.

'*Señorita*, I have your letter to Señor Hardin. I do not know if the address I have for him is any good. It was one given long ago; he may have moved.'

Molly's spirits dropped. She had so counted on Miguel knowing how to contact him.

'Send it to the address you have. If he has moved, perhaps they will forward it. Thank you, Miguel.' She hung up. Now it was only a matter of time. Time and luck that the address was correct.

The work on the book was drawing to an end. Molly could tell from the events taking place that General Pershing was drawing near the end of his career. Beverley dictated tirelessly, and Molly's fingers flew to keep up. With the end in sight, there was all the more reason to keep on.

Beverley walked in very solemnly one morning and stood beside Molly. Dramatically she handed the tape to her secretary.

'The last one!' she said.

'Already? It's gone by so fast,' Molly murmured, taking the tape.

'Yes, but I had it mapped out before the actual dictating. I knew as I was doing the research how I would tell his life. And this is only the first draft. We still have weeks of work left. But I'm glad this is over. I feel drained.' Beverley wandered out to the patio.

Molly inserted the tape into the machine. Now she could see the final scenes of Black Jack's life, and the wrap-up that Beverley was known for. There was still editing and re-writes to be done, but the major effort of the book was complete. Molly felt excited to see the end. The re-writes and polishing was still ahead, but she'd at least know the ending.

She finished the last page just before dinner.

Beverley was sitting on the patio, gazing out over the bay, a stiff drink in her hand.

'I'm done. It's wonderful, Beverley.' Molly plopped in the chair beside her, her praise honest.

'Thank you. We'll leave in the morning,' Beverley said, smiling at her secretary.

'Leave? For where?'

'Home. I just got a call from my sister. She figured I should be about finished now and wants me to stop by before returning to LA. I told her we'd leave in the morning, stay a few days with her then return to LA. Still lots to do on this book before I can submit it, but the next part is the grinding part. We'll lock ourselves up in my place at Malibu and work day and night until it's done.'

'But...I thought we'd stay here a little longer.' Panic touched Molly. Tell didn't know where she lived. If she left here, how would he reach her? She'd been hoping daily for some word from him. She couldn't just disappear. Quickly her mind sorted through ideas. She'd have to send him another letter, letting him know of the change of plans. If she'd only suspected Beverley would leave so precipitately she'd have included her home address in her letter. It had been a week. Had he even received her letter yet? Had he changed his mind? Or was his letter to her even now on its way back?

'No need to stay. I've finished the book, you've finished the tapes, pack up tonight. Tomorrow we leave on the ten a.m. flight. Where shall we go for our last night in Acapulco?'

Molly must have given an answer because Beverley rose to get dressed, but she didn't remember speaking. Her thoughts were whirling. She'd have to write to Tell immediately, and wished she knew where to reach him. Wished she would still be in Acapulco when he contacted her. Now she'd have to wait another week or so before she could possibly hear from him. Blast. Each day was like an eternity. It could be weeks before she'd get his answer. She wanted to hear from him now!

They ate at one of the seaside restaurants on the beach. The scampi was delicious, but Molly scarcely tasted it. She was absorbing every last sight she could of Acapulco. It was her last night in this magical paradise and she wanted to remember it, whatever happened. Acapulco was the place where she'd fallen in love.

She remembered Tell's last night, and wished she'd found the courage to accept him when he'd asked her to come away, wished she could have seen him again before he left. Wished she'd been brave enough to agree to go with him then, though she would have stayed through the end of the book. She owed Beverley that much.

She packed quickly when they reached their rooms, and hastily drafted another letter to Tell. In the morning she'd leave it with Miguel. He'd mail it for her and Tell could be calling her by the time she reached LA. She'd forgotten to ask Beverley where her sister lived—if it was California, maybe Molly needn't stay and could be home by supper.

They stopped at the desk next morning to drop off their keys and turn in the gaily coloured blue and white jeep. A taxi was taking them to the airport. Molly took the opportunity to look for Miguel. He was not on duty, Carlos was.

Molly's heart sank.

'Is Miguel coming in today?' she asked, glancing over her shoulder to make sure she was not holding Beverley up.

'No, *señorita*, it is his day off; he will return in two days. Can I help you?'

'Do you know Señor Hardin?'

'No, I do not believe I know the *señor*. Is he registered here?'

'No. I . . . he's not even in Mexico any more. He lives in Texas. Miguel knows where. I wanted to send him a letter.'

'I'm sorry, *señorita*, I do not know him.'

'Could I leave the letter for Miguel to send?'

'*Sí*, I will tell him.'

Dissatisfied with the way things were going, Molly had no choice but to hand over the envelope, with a few pesos for postage. She smiled her thanks and hurried to join Beverley as the taxi pulled up.

Down the Carretera Escénica, Acapulco Bay behind them. Soon they crested the last hill and the sight of the beautiful city was lost from view. Along this road Molly and Tell had driven to reach the Revolcadero Beach, to ride the horses. Her eyes filled with tears. She'd been so happy that day. Until his announcement that night shattered her serenity. Despite her accusations and suspicions, he had wanted her to come with him. She wished she had said yes.

Past the turn-off, the beautiful Acapulco Princess, the pyramid hotel rising from the beach on their right. On the taxi sped, to the airport.

Molly gazed at the scene with sadness. Would her letters reach Tell? Would he want to see her after she'd so adamantly refused him when he'd first asked her to come with him? What if he didn't want her any more? How would she stand that?

She was numb when they climbed aboard the sleek jet. They found their seats, and then she gazed out of the window at the brown hills of Mexico. In only minutes they would be leaving and her one touch with Tell gone. Please let Miguel have his correct address, she prayed.

The take-off was uneventful. Molly watched as they circled Acapulco Bay one last time and headed north. She settled back to read another mystery that she'd bought at the airport, wondering where they were going and how long they would stay. After endless moments without reading a single word, she gave up.

'Where does your sister live?' she asked Beverley as that lady bustled about in her seat, trying to get comfortable, she said.

'Texas. We're flying into Dallas, then we'll get a connecting flight to Laredo. We'll be met there, driven to the ranch.'

'Ranch?'

'Mmm, Sally lives on a ranch. I come from that area. Raised there. Tell will probably pick us up; he lives closest to the airport.'

'Tell?'

A strange feeling started in Molly. She felt as if she were near a momentous discovery, her heartbeat sped up. She turned to stare at Beverley.

'Tell Hardin. You met him in Acapulco one day.'

'Yes, you—er—warned me away from him.' Molly was trying to make sense of this. 'Do you know him from Texas?'

'Honey, I've known him all his life—he's my nephew, Sally's oldest boy.'

Molly was thunderstruck. She stared at Beverley, almost unable to believe her ears, her mind scrambling to make sense of this turn.

'Tell Hardin is your *nephew*? But you told me he was nothing but trouble.'

'Oh, he is that, all right. Trouble for any pretty young girl. He likes girls. They like him, too. He's always fending them off. But he's a hot-headed, wild kid. Comes from having so much money, spending it, being sought after for his money, I guess. He doesn't cotton to any kind of commitment, or long-term relationship. Twice I've thought he was close, but the girls just wanted the money. He's been burned so I doubt he'll ever marry. You're too nice to be taken in by Tell. That's why I warned you away. You're too naïve and proper for the likes of him. He'd be nothing but trouble for someone like you.'

Tell had thought her proper, too. He'd often teased her about it. Yet he'd asked her to come away with him. *But with no mention of marriage.*

'He has money?' Why hadn't he told her? Had he just been toying with her, as Beverley suggested? He knew security was important to her; why hadn't he told her?

'Sure, though you would never guess from the way he carries on in Mexico. He likes to camp rather than stay in one of the hotels, dresses like a beach bum and goes to cheap restaurants. Says it's his way to get

with real people again. I'd like to know what he thinks
his family is made of—fake people? Jim, that's their
dad, he gave them each some cash to start off with.
Tell's done well with his share, bought a ranch, even
makes money at it, too.'

'So he owns the ranch, doesn't just work there,'
Molly said, almost to herself.

'He works darn hard. But he also has a strong
feeling for family. That's why he was down in
Acapulco, looking out for me. Sally told him I was
going there and so he dropped by to make sure I was
doing OK. Really, my family acts as if I can't get on
myself. Anyway, I only saw him once. He must have
gone home after that.'

No, he hadn't, Molly sighed softly. But it might
have been better if he had.

'I don't know why Sally wants me to stop by, but
she rarely asks for anything, so I might as well visit
her. We'll just delay polishing the book for a few days.
You'll like their place, out in the hills, beautiful
country, not a bit like LA. Though I like LA.'

Molly stared out of the window, her thoughts
spinning. She could scarcely take it all in. It was the
furthest thing from her mind when she started the
flight. She'd been so distraught to be leaving before
contacting Tell; now it looked as if she would be seeing
him in a few hours.

Trust me, he'd said. She smiled; she had trusted in
him. She'd decided to follow him before she knew
who he was, before she knew he could offer her the
security and stability she craved. She'd trusted her
heart and offered her commitment before she knew.

Her heart beat faster and a loving smile touched
her face, grew. She'd be seeing him soon, and every-

thing would be all right. She'd be able to tell him in person how much she loved him. Had he been glad when he read her letter? Was it really his mother who had arranged their visit, or Tell through his mother?

Molly could hardly wait. The depression of the last few days disappeared instantly. She would see him again, soon.

They had a brief stop-over in Dallas, and Molly took the time to make sure her make-up was fresh and her hair combed. Excited about the upcoming meeting, she was impatient with the delay but tried to hide it from Beverley. She wore the suit she'd travelled to Mexico in, the one Tell had seen her in the first night on the patio. Would he remember it? She wished she could have worn one of her new blouses and a pair of shorts, but this was more appropriate for travel.

The short flight from Dallas to Laredo was soon over, and Molly and Beverley entered the air-conditioned airport building. Scanning the waiting people, Molly's heart sped up when she spotted Tell's tall figure, standing a bit behind the crowd, tall, arrogant, standing apart from the others. His eyes clashed with hers.

She smiled and waved, happiness bubbling up, love shining from her face. But his glance was enigmatic, his expression non-committal. He didn't smile back, his eyes narrowed and he looked as if he was considering what to say. Her heart skipped a beat. He looked wonderful. She was so glad to see him again.

He was as tall as ever, dressed in tight jeans and a blue and white checked shirt. He wore cowboy boots and in his hand a cowboy hat. Molly feasted her eyes on him, her own love shining out.

'Hello, Tell,' she said shyly as they approached.

He nodded, leaning over to kiss his aunt on her cheek. 'Hello, Beverley, Molly.'

'Well, what does your mother need that I have to come all the way over here for a visit? Couldn't she come visit me in LA?' Beverley asked, looking up at her tall nephew.

'You'll have to ask her, ma'am. I just came to pick you up.' His eyes never left Molly's. But he didn't seem happy to see her. Not the way she felt. She wondered if they would get to have some privacy soon. Maybe he didn't want to speak before his aunt. He must have received her letter; had she been too bold? Doubts crowded her mind. Had it been only the wine and the moonlight talking? Had it only been a holiday fling, one he didn't want known by his family?

'Ready?'

Molly nodded and moved to Beverley's far side. She didn't understand; why wasn't Tell happier to see her? He'd asked her to come away with him; had he changed his mind? Uncertainty began to build.

She wished now that she had not come with Beverley. She should have insisted she return home, to wait for Beverley there. To wait for Tell's letter. How awkward it would be if he didn't want her. Colour washed in her face, as she avoided looking at him.

Molly and Beverley had to walk quickly through the airport to keep up with Tell's longer stride. He fetched their luggage and soon had it stowed in his large pick-up truck.

'You sit in the middle, Molly, I want the window.' Beverley paused at the door.

Tell's lips tightened, but he said nothing as Molly slid across the seat. After closing the door behind Beverley, he went around and climbed in.

His leg was only inches from Molly's and she could feel the heat radiating from it in the hot afternoon. His arm brushed hers as he turned the wheel. She pulled slightly away, puzzled by his reaction, her arm tingling at his touch. Was he mad? Did he not want to speak to her in front of Beverley?

'How are your folks?' Beverley asked as they gained the highway.

'Doing well. Diane is home with the baby. Ellie will be over on the weekend. How long are you staying?' Tell asked, ignoring Molly.

'Don't know. Depends on your mother. I've finished the draft of the book, might as well take a few days off before starting in on the polishing. You know I like to do all that at one sitting. Go on back to LA for that. Be glad to see the baby, bet he's grown since I saw him last.'

The talk continued over Molly, about the family, the friends in the area who Beverley kept up with. Molly kept her gaze in front, watching the road, fascinated by her first sight of Texas. All the while, however, she was intensely conscious of Tell beside her, his body only inches away, his strong hands gripping the steering-wheel. Conscious of the fact he hadn't seemed glad to see her. What was wrong—did he think she didn't want Beverley to know? She felt guilty about their last night. But she couldn't say anything now. Maybe when they were alone. Surely they'd be able to manage a few minutes alone.

Tell turned off the highway on to a secondary road. Soon he turned again on to a long black-top driveway, the wire fences on either side keeping the grazing cattle from straying on the road. Molly watched as they drove into a large farmyard, where a huge old-fashioned farmhouse with a wide covered porch stood in the middle. Tell stopped the truck and hopped out.

Opening the door for his aunt, he helped her down, then stood looking at Molly. She slid across the seat, her skirt riding up a little with the friction. She flushed and tried to pull it down. His hand caught hers and held it a moment, then tugged gently, helping her down from the high cab. Her fingers gripped his, but he pulled away.

'Beverley, so glad you could come.' A salt-and-pepper-haired woman hurried from the house and gave Beverley a big hug. She was not much taller than her sister. Turning, she gave Molly a bright smile of welcome.

'This is Molly Spencer, my secretary. Molly, my sister Sally Hardin,' Beverley introduced them.

'Welcome, Molly. Tell, why don't you take Molly's and Beverley's bags up, show Molly her room?' His mother gave him a pat on his arm and moved with her sister to the front porch, already talking about the grandchildren, and who would be at dinner that evening.

Tell pulled Molly's suitcases from the back of the truck and climbed the few stairs to the porch.

'If you'll open the door, we'll go right up the stairs.' He waited for Molly to hold the screen door for him, then led the way. Molly followed behind him, feeling lost and overwhelmed.

He climbed the stairs leading to the second floor, then walked easily down the hall to the last bedroom on the right. Pushing open the door, he entered and dumped her bags by the bed. Molly followed.

'What are you doing here?' Tell asked in a hard voice as he straightened, and reached around Molly to close the door.

Her heart began beating erratically, colour rose in her cheeks. 'You weren't surprised to see me?' She stalled for time.

'No, I knew you were coming. More to the point, you weren't surprised to see me.'

'Beverley told me who you were.'

'I see.'

Molly peeked up at his face, growing chilled at the hard look. 'Tell?'

'What?' He stared down at her, his eyes slate-grey, a muscle jerked in his cheek.

'I'm glad to see you,' she said in a small voice.

When he said nothing, her heart dropped; she was so puzzled. What had she done wrong?

Molly glanced around the room. It was pleasantly decorated in bright crisp cotton prints at the window and on the bed. The hardwood floor shone, and the braided rug by the bed caught the colours from the spread.

She took a breath and looked at him again. 'You said if I changed my mind to let you know.'

'You were always to the point, Molly. You wanted a man with money. Is that why you're glad to see me now?'

'No!' She stepped back, came up against the closed door. 'I wanted to see you before I knew you had any money. I asked Miguel to let you know. He said you'd already gone. I . . . I sent a letter.'

'Good try, Molly. No letter. How long have you known I was not the destitute cowboy you thought?'

'Beverley told me on the plane.' Molly was growing sick to her stomach. Things were not going the way she'd thought they would. Tell was looking at her as if he disliked her. Where was the fun-loving, carefree man she'd known in Acapulco? The man who had urged her to come away with him?

'So everything is perfect. You find the man with money enough to keep you secure, and I get the girl, is that it?'

She shook her head slowly, staring at him with wide, frightened eyes. 'You asked me to come with you,' she whispered.

'Too right. I wanted you to come to me not knowing that I had some money. I wanted you to trust me, want me for myself, not as a free meal ticket. It was important to me, Molly. I want to be wanted for myself, not because I have money.'

'I do want you for yourself, Tell!'

'Since when?'

'Since before you left, all along, only I didn't realise it. Once you were gone, I knew how much I missed you, how much I loved you, how much I wanted to be with you, have you with me. I wrote you, days ago. Beverley only told me you were her nephew on the plane today.'

'Seems too opportune to me,' he ground out.

'It's the truth.'

'I'll never know now, will I?'

'Ask Beverley, she can tell you.'

He gently set her aside and opened the door. In two strides he had gained the hall and left.

Molly stood where he'd placed her, shock on her face. She'd come and he didn't want her. He didn't believe she loved him, only that she wanted him because he had money. Tears welled and spilled over.

CHAPTER TWELVE

MOLLY heard Tell's footsteps as he walked down the hall, the hard heels of his boots hitting the stairs, growing fainter until she no longer heard him. The tears fell in earnest and she moved to the bed, sitting on the edge, her face in her hands.

He didn't want her. After all was said and done, he didn't want her here. Who would have thought anything could hurt like this? Her heart felt as if it would break. That night on the boat had been awful, but this was worse! After everything, he thought she only wanted his money and he didn't want her on those terms. Couldn't he trust in her?

She heard his footsteps again and quickly dashed the tears from her eyes, brushed her cheeks. Rising, she walked over to her window and looked out over the rolling land. She could see the cattle grazing in the afternoon sun. In the distance a tall windmill was silhouetted against the horizon. It was too far to see if it was stirring in any breeze.

Was he coming back to talk to her? Was it some awful joke?

He came down the hall, pausing near her door, then walking away. Delivering Beverley's suitcases, most likely, Molly thought dully. She looked longingly at the bed. She'd like to crawl in and cover her head and shut out the world. But she couldn't. She was a guest in the house of Tell's mother and had to follow conventions no matter how hard.

She smiled sadly. She was a proper young woman, as he'd said, doing what was right no matter how she felt. Slipping off her jacket, she peered into the mirror. Her face looked hot and tear-stained.

Opening her door quietly, she peered out and found the hall empty. She found the bathroom across the hall and down two doors. She washed her face and applied make-up with a light hand. She had to venture forward, though she found it hard. Would Tell be staying? Or would he return to his ranch now that he'd picked up the visitors?

She suddenly wanted to see him again. Didn't want him to leave before she could... Could what? Talk to him? Explain? Get him to listen to her? *Make* him listen to her! In front of everyone who was around? Molly slowed her pace. She couldn't do it.

Slowly she descended the stairs. Voices and snatches of conversations drifted in from the opened front door. People were on the large porch. Shyly she pushed open the screen door and stepped outside.

'Come and sit over here, Molly,' Beverley called to her. 'We have some lemonade or iced tea, whichever you prefer. Come and see my great-nephew. And my other greats.'

Beverley motioned to one of several rocking-chairs on the wooden porch, most of which were filled. Molly smiled and walked over. Tell was at the far side, balancing a young boy on his knee, rocking him back and forth and talking to him. His eyes were on Molly and narrowed as he watched her cross the porch.

She stumbled and sank gratefully into the chair.

'I'm Diane, Beverley's niece. And these wild kids are mine. The baby's Brandon, the young man with Uncle Tell is Thomas, and that sassy girl is Sue-Anne.' Tell's sister resembled him, with her dark hair and

light eyes. She smiled in a friendly fashion at Molly.
The baby was held so that Beverley could see him.

Sue-Anne was about two and talking a blue streak
to her grandmother. Molly smiled and looked over to
Thomas, who was having a wonderful time with his
uncle. Her eyes met Tell's again, and she jerked away.
It was strange to see him in a family setting. Her
thoughts of him had always been quite different.

'How did you like Acapulco?' Sally asked, handing
Molly lemonade.

'Very much. It's a beautiful place.'

'Boring, though, for a single girl who has to work
there, I dare say,' Beverley commented. 'But Molly
was good, she never complained.'

'And were you bored?' Tell spoke from across the
porch, his eyes boring into hers, the mocking light
evident.

Her hands shook a little, and she took a quick sip
of lemonade. How dared he mock her in front of
everyone where she couldn't answer back? If they were
alone she'd tell him something that would make his
ears burn. She glared at him and turned away before
anyone else could see her expression. Schooling her
voice, she said, 'I wasn't bored. The work was interesting and I saw some of the sights in my time off.
Met some of the local characters.' Her voice was low,
controlled, and she refused to be cowed by him.

'I had hoped Luis would be able to show her
around, but he had to spend time in Mexico City.
Molly only saw him a couple of times,' Beverley explained to her sister.

'Old family friends, Molly. Did you like Luis?'

'Yes, he was very pleasant.' Old family friends—
had that been Tell at the party that night? Had he
deliberately made sure she wouldn't see him there?

But why? Was he ashamed to be with her? She was all right for a holiday fling, but not to acknowledge to his family or friends?

She felt Tell's eyes on her, still. But she refused to look his way, watching the ice cubes in her glass instead.

'I was sorry Luis was away so much. They did go on the dinner cruise, but I was working so hard on the book that I guess I didn't allow for much time off for you, Molly,' Beverley said.

'But I bet you *honestly* had a good time on the cruise with Luis, didn't you?' Tell's voice was silky.

She threw him a look and glanced away. He was being hateful. Hateful and hurtful. 'I enjoyed the evening,' she said softly, not trusting herself to look at him, not wanting to remember that evening. She'd hated it when she'd learned he was leaving. That evening had changed everything.

'*Trust me*,' Tell continued, setting little Thomas on his feet. 'I'm sure every outing you had with Luis would be enjoyable. He'd give anyone a strong, secure feeling.'

Molly flinched as if she'd been struck. Why was he being so hurtful to her? She'd turned him down, and when she'd changed her mind, as he had indicated she could, he refused to have anything to do with her. If he didn't want her, then why not just leave her alone?

'Tell——'

'Sorry, Mom. I've got to go. Things to do.' He rose and started down the shallow wooden stairs.

'Aren't you staying to dinner?'

'No, another time. Goodbye, everyone.' His eyes skimmed the porch, held Molly's a moment, then moved on.

She watched him as he got into his truck, started it and drove off, gravel spurting from beneath the tyres. She watched down the drive long after the truck had disappeared from view. Depression cloaked her and time seemed to stand still.

The rest of the afternoon passed like none Molly had ever known. The Hardin family drew her in as if she were one of them. She played with the children, helped Diane change Brandon, and when it was time for dinner she offered to help. It was the right thing to do. All the women joined in to prepare the evening meal and Molly felt a camaraderie with the others that she had never known while growing up. Everyone liked each other and the stories and conversations changed and flowed non-stop.

There were more people to sit at the table than Molly had ever seen at one family group. Jim Hardin, an older version of Tell, headed the table. Diane and her husband, Beverley, Tell's cousin Jack and his friend Marc, the children and Sally. These were the people he'd told her about in Acapulco. She felt as if she knew them already, and liked them. It was a lively group and Molly had no time to brood or worry about Tell. Surprisingly, she was enjoying herself, though she wished briefly that Tell was there, too.

Helping with the dishes afterwards kept her from thinking, dreaming. She was pleasantly tired by the time the kitchen was put to rights. It had been a long day for her. The men drifted to the living-room, engrossed in a ball game on the television. Diane had taken the kids upstairs to get ready for bed, and Sally and Beverley settled at the kitchen table with coffee for a cosy conversation.

Molly wandered out to the porch. The night was still, the sounds of cicadas in the background a soothing cadence in the warm night air, the soft murmur of the television a reminder of others near by. The only illumination was that spilling out from the windows and the door. In the night sky, the stars shone with brilliance not seen from city streets. It was lovely.

In the distance, Molly could see the rolling hills give way to the star-studded sky. She leaned against the railing and thought of the view in Acapulco. This didn't compare, but it was pretty in its own way, enchanting, yet calm, peaceful, and serene.

She heard the step on the gravel at the side of the house and turned. Tell came around the corner, pausing when he saw her on the porch.

She smiled involuntarily, memory flashing back.

'The first time I saw you I thought you were a Mexican bandit,' she said softly, remembering that first night.

He vaulted the railing on the side, dropped something on a chair and walked over to her, his boots sounding loud on the wooden porch.

'And I thought you were Aunt Beverley's very prim and proper new secretary. Trying so hard to get rid of the riff-raff.' He stopped beside her. Molly had to tilt back her head to see him. Her breathing was constricted. Why had he returned?

'The view here's not quite the same,' he said softly, turning to look out over the rolling fields, the star-studded night sky.

'No, but still pretty.'

'Still pretty,' he echoed and his head came down, blotting out the stars.

His lips were warm and gentle when they first touched hers, but soon they hardened, moved, demanding, seeking and finding a response from her.

She opened her mouth and tasted him, tasted the sweet assault of his tongue as it invaded her, sparking her to life. Her tongue duelled with his, followed it to his mouth, emotions exploding as she spiralled higher and higher.

Only their mouths touched, and Molly thought she'd float away. Every nerve-ending longed for his touch, but she held herself away; the delight and rapture of his kiss made further contact unnecessary. She thought she couldn't go any higher, but she wished he'd hold her.

Tell's hands gripped her shoulders and gently moved her back, breaking contact.

She blinked up at him, disappointment flooding through her.

Leaning back against the railing, his legs spread apart, Tell brought her around before him, pulling her into the confines of his legs, staring down at her in the faint starlight.

'Still prim and proper?' he asked.

'I don't feel prim or proper,' she replied, her breathing ragged.

He moved his hand to her blouse, slowly unfastening the top button, the second, the third. She thought instantly of the night in his tent. She'd felt so wanton then, and now. The dark shadow between her breasts was revealed, and he stared down at her, dropping his hands to hers, lacing his fingers through hers.

'If you don't feel prim or proper, how do you feel?' he asked softly.

'Very daring, actually,' she replied promptly, looking up to see him. His face was in shadow, but she knew he was looking at her.

'Why?'

'This is all daring for me. I . . . I feel I threw everything over on a gamble. I don't usually gamble. And it looks as if I lost anyway.'

'What gamble?'

'I told you, I changed my mind, and I wrote you to tell you. I didn't know you weren't a broke, drifting cowboy until the plane ride this morning, when Beverley told me. Ask her, if you don't believe me.'

'So you were coming to me thinking I had no money.' He swung their linked hands slightly, Molly aware of every inch of his roughened hands against hers.

'You said to trust you, Tell. I thought about nothing else after you left. Life was miserable for me. So I decided to trust in you. Trust that you would do the best you could for me, for us. And I wrote you,' she said simply.

'Trust,' he repeated.

'Yes.' She paused, trying to see him in the starlight. Their future was at stake. 'I trusted in you Tell; why can't you trust in me? I love you. I risked everything I had in that letter—all my pride, my feeling of self-worth. I can't help it if you didn't get it. I trusted in you. Can't you trust in me?'

His hands tightened on hers and he slowly pulled her into his arms, his head resting on hers. 'I have to, Molly. I learned that this afternoon. When you got off the plane, clearly expecting to see someone, and not a bit surprised when you saw me, I knew you knew I had money. You seemed so . . . so happy, like you'd found the gold at the end of the rainbow. I thought the money was the reason for your change. I was engaged once before, to a woman I thought was wonderful, only to find out a few months before the wedding that she was mainly interested in my money and my prospects. Not me.'

Molly's arms tightened around him. How awful to be wanted for money. How could any woman not want him for himself alone?

'That's why I was so careful in Acapulco,' he went on. 'I wanted to be sure it was me, not anything else that attracted you. And all I got was how you wanted someone with money.'

'But it is you I want, Tell. I don't care about the money. Not any more. I just want to be with you, stay with you, love you.'

'Then stay with me forever, my heart's delight. Marry me, and stay right here in Texas with me forever.'

His kiss was hard and possessive, and Molly loved it. Her heart soared and the happiness she felt threatened to explode. She saw stars, but were they from the dark Texas sky or the love of Tell Hardin? Her pulse increased as the blood raced through her veins. Her heart pounded, or was it his? She was where she wanted to be, in Tell's arms.

When Tell pulled back, Molly was trembling. She longed for more kisses, for more explanations, to hear that Tell loved her.

But he took her arm and hurried her across the porch, down the steps and across the yard.

'Where are we going?' she asked, searching the barnyard in the faint light.

'My place. I don't intend to wait for the wedding to make love to you, and I sure can't do it before under my mother's roof.' His voice was low, rough with emotion.

'But what will everyone think?' she protested.

'They'll think you've gone to bed now, and I'll bring you back early in the morning, before anyone is up.'

'I don't have any clothes,' she pointed out.

'I have some jeans that you can wear. I'm sorry you don't have your bathing suit with you. I like you in that outfit.'

The memory of their ride along the beach brought warmth to her heart. That had been such a happy day.

'And tomorrow we can plan our wedding,' he told her.

'Beverley's book. I have to help her finish it.'

'She can do it here in Texas. You can help her with it as long as she stays here.'

Molly smiled as he opened the door to the truck and helped her inside; he was taking over again. And she didn't mind at all.

She slid across the seat to sit next to Tell as he drove through the dark Texas night. His hand rested on her knee, slid between her thighs and gently massaged. Molly could hardly think straight and wondered how he could drive if he felt at all the way she did.

'Lord, sweetheart, I've been miserable today. I thought you only came because you found out about the money.'

'You don't think that any more, do you?' She was anxious to clear that up. She didn't want that standing between them forever.

'No. I believe what you told me. I wish you'd told me before I left Mexico. Do you know what these last few weeks have been like?'

'Awful! I know because I lived through them, too,' she said, snuggling closer, almost afraid to believe Tell loved her, wanting to touch him to reassure herself he was real.

'Hellish, more like it. Do you want a big wedding?'

'No. I have no family, few friends. I'd just as soon get married quietly,' she confessed.

'And quickly.'

And quickly, her heart sang. It had come right. Trusting in Tell had proved the right thing to do.

As the truck raced swiftly through the night, Tell spoke again. 'I kept hoping you would show up, at the camp, or at the airport. I had to get back, but I didn't want to leave you behind. I had to know you wanted me, though. You always talked about wanting money.'

'I had hoped you would come one more time,' she admitted. 'Every time I went on the patio, I looked for you. When I finally went to see Miguel, I couldn't believe you had really left without seeing me again.'

'Would your answer have been different?' he asked.

'I think so, if you had talked to me again. A lot of the reason I changed my mind was because of the things you had said.'

'Hold on a second.' He turned into another long driveway, stopping by the mailbox. Grabbing the stack in the box, he handed it to Molly, starting the truck again.

'I missed you dreadfully. Everything I did or saw reminded me of you,' she said softly, her hand on his jeans-clad thigh. 'Acapulco was no longer enchanting with you gone.'

'I was mad at first that you wouldn't go with me.'

'You didn't ask me to marry you, not then,' she reminded him.

'I don't think I was thinking that far, only that I wanted you with me. I realised once I got home that I wanted you with me forever. I almost went back on the next plane.'

'What if I hadn't come with Beverley?' Molly was suddenly frightened at the thought of how close they had come to not being together, to not admitting they loved each other.

'I hadn't expected her before my mother told me yesterday. I had planned to look you up in LA, see if I could fan the fire I thought was building.'

She smiled and rested her head on his shoulder. The fire threatened to consume her; he had no need to fan it.

Tell stopped before a low, rambling ranch house, more modern than that of his parents. There was a veranda to the side, and large picture windows to see the land.

'Do that cute trick where your skirt rides up when you get out,' he suggested, the teasing light back in his grey eyes.

She laughed. With her skirt riding up, and her blouse unbuttoned to her bra, she no longer felt the proper young woman she'd been when she first met Tell.

He reached for her with a groan and Molly started to fall into his arms, but the flash of blue colour from the corner of her eye stopped her.

She looked at the stack of mail. There, protruding from beneath a farm journal, was her letter.

'Tell, my letter!' She drew it from the stack and held it out to him. 'Look at the postmark; this will prove to you I changed my mind before I knew about your money, that I came for you alone.'

He took the unopened letter and put it in his pocket, reaching for Molly.

'Thank you, sweetheart, but I already knew that. Welcome home, Molly.' And he swept her into his arms and carried her into the darkened house.

Next Month's Romances

Each month you can choose from a wide variety of romance with Mills & Boon. Below are the new titles to look out for next month, why not ask either Mills & Boon Reader Service or your Newsagent to reserve you a copy of the titles you want to buy – just tick the titles you would like and either post to Reader Service or take it to any Newsagent and ask them to order your books.

Please save me the following titles:	Please tick	√
SIMPLY IRRESISTIBLE	Miranda Lee	
HUNTER'S MOON	Carole Mortimer	
AT ODDS WITH LOVE	Betty Neels	
A DANGEROUS MAGIC	Patricia Wilson	
TOWER OF SHADOWS	Sara Craven	
THE UNMARRIED BRIDE	Emma Goldrick	
SWEET BETRAYAL	Helen Brooks	
COUNTERFEIT LOVE	Stephanie Howard	
A TEMPORARY AFFAIR	Kate Proctor	
SHADES OF SIN	Sara Wood	
RUTHLESS STRANGER	Margaret Mayo	
BITTERSWEET LOVE	Cathy Williams	
CAPTIVE BRIDE	Rosemary Carter	
WILLING OR NOT	Liza Hadley	
MASTER OF NAMANGILLA	Mons Daveson	
LOVE YOUR ENEMY	Ellen James	
A FOOLISH HEART	Laura Martin	

If you would like to order these books in addition to your regular subscription from Mills & Boon Reader Service please send £1.80 per title to: Mills & Boon Reader Service, Freepost, P.O. Box 236, Croydon, Surrey, CR9 9EL, quote your Subscriber No:.................................. (If applicable) and complete the name and address details below. Alternatively, these books are available from many local Newsagents including W.H.Smith, J.Menzies, Martins and other paperback stockists from 13 August 1993.

Name:..

Address:...

....Post Code:.........................

To Retailer: If you would like to stock M&B books please contact your regular book/magazine wholesaler for details.

You may be mailed with offers from other reputable companies as a result of this application. If you would rather not take advantage of these opportunities please tick box ☐

4 FREE

Romances and 2 FREE gifts just for you!

*You can enjoy all the
heartwarming emotion of true love for FREE!
Discover the heartbreak and happiness,
the emotion and the tenderness of the modern
relationships in Mills & Boon Romances.*

*We'll send you 4 Romances as a special offer
from Mills & Boon Reader Service,
along with the opportunity to have 6 captivating
new Romances delivered to your door each month.*

Claim your FREE books and gifts overleaf...

An irresistible offer from Mills & Boon

Become a regular reader of Romances with Mills & Boon Reader Service and we'll welcome you with 4 books, a CUDDLY TEDDY and a special MYSTERY GIFT all absolutely FREE.

And then look forward to receiving 6 brand new Romances each month, delivered to your door hot off the presses, postage and packing FREE! Plus our free Newsletter featuring author news, competitions, special offers and much more.

This invitation comes with no strings attached. You may cancel or suspend your subscription at any time, and still keep your free books and gifts.

It's so easy. Send no money now. Simply fill in the coupon below and post it to -
Reader Service, FREEPOST, PO Box 236, Croydon, Surrey CR9 9EL.

NO STAMP REQUIRED

Free Books Coupon

Yes! Please rush me 4 FREE Romances and 2 FREE gifts! Please also reserve me a Reader Service subscription. If I decide to subscribe I can look forward to receiving 6 brand new Romances for just £10.80 each month, postage and packing FREE. If I decide not to subscribe I shall write to you within 10 days - I can keep the free books and gifts whatever I choose. I may cancel or suspend my subscription at any time. I am over 18 years of age.

Ms/Mrs/Miss/Mr _____ EP56R

Address _____

_____

Postcode _____ Signature _____